The Sisters Club

Megan McDonald is the
author of the immensely popular Judy Moody series
and its companion series starring Judy's brother, Stink.
She is also the author of *Ant and Honey Bee: What a Pair!*,
a picture book illustrated by G. Brian Karas. The youngest
of five sisters, Megan McDonald lives in
northern California.

You can find out more about Megan McDonald
and her books at **www.meganmcdonald.net**

Books by the same author

Judy Moody
Judy Moody Gets Famous!
Judy Moody Saves the World!
Judy Moody Predicts the Future
Doctor Judy Moody
Judy Moody Declares Independence!
Judy Moody Around the World in 8½ Days
Judy Moody Goes to College
The Judy Moody Mood Journal
Judy Moody's Double-Rare Way-Not-Boring
Book of Fun Stuff to Do
Judy Moody's Way Wacky Uber Awesome Book of More
Fun Stuff to Do
Stink: The Incredible Shrinking Kid
Stink and the Incredible Super-Galactic Jawbreaker
Stink and the World's Worst Super-Stinky Sneakers
Stink and the Great Guinea Pig Express
Judy Moody & Stink: The Holly Joliday
Ant and Honey Bee: What a Pair!

The Sisters Club

Rule of Three

Megan McDonald

WALKER
BOOKS

First published in Great Britain 2010 by Walker Books Ltd
87 Vauxhall Walk, London SE11 5HJ

2 4 6 8 10 9 7 5 3 1

Text © 2009 Megan McDonald
Illustrations © 2009 Pamela A. Consolazio
Cover photograph © Foodfolio/Alamy
Cover design by Walker Books Ltd

"The Glory of Love" written by Billy Hill. Used by permission of Shapiro, Bernstein & Co., Inc.
International copyright secured.

The right of Megan McDonald and Pamela A. Consolazio to be identified as author and illustrator respectively of this work has been asserted by them in accordance with the Copyright, Designs and Patents Act 1988

This book has been typeset in Cheltenham, Kidprint and Passport

Printed and bound in Great Britain by Clays Ltd, St Ives plc

British Library Cataloguing in Publication Data:
a catalogue record for this book is available from the British Library

ISBN 978-1-4063-2473-0

www.walker.co.uk

For my own Sisters Club—
Suzy, Deb, Michele, Missy

Me, Myself, I

Knife, fork, spoon.

Rock, paper, scissors.

Lights, camera, action.

Everywhere you look, things come in threes. It's the Rule of Three.

Honest. It's a real rule. The Rule of Three says that things are better when they come in threes.

Think about it: red, white, blue. Snap, crackle, pop. Bacon, lettuce, tomato.

I'm in the middle of three. Sisters, that is. There's Alex, oldest and (still!) bossiest; and Joey, youngest and not really a pest anymore, except for when it comes to *Little Women*.

And me. *Me, Myself, and I.* Stevie (not Steven!) Reel.

My dad used to be an actor, and he teaches classes and workshops in drama. He says most plays have a three-act structure. Act I, Act II, Act III. Introduction, Confrontation, Resolution. Dad calls it some fancy name, like Aristotle's Incline or something. But really it just means Beginning, Middle, End.

Once you start to pay attention, you find threes everywhere.

They started popping up in science class:

Solid, liquid, gas.

Crust, mantle, core.

Igneous, metamorphic, sedimentary. It even works for rocks.

Columbus had three ships. Space has three dimensions. Even Plato said the soul has three parts. The whole world is made up of threes!

Believe it or not, you can find rules of three in math, myth, and music; in plants, animals, and nature; in art and in architecture.

See? I am not making this up. It's a real rule (not a Reel rule!). Like an actual law of the universe or something.

What goes up must come down.

For every action, there is an equal and opposite reaction.

Anything that can go wrong will go wrong.

With three sisters, we know all about stuff going wrong. But at least it's not boring. That's what my best friend, Olivia, says.

She's an Only. She's always going on about how lucky I am to be in a family of three sisters. I try to get it through her head—lots of times, sisters are like … well, like this magnet Joey has stuck on her bulletin board: *Big sisters are the crabgrass in the lawn of life.*

Olivia doesn't know about the crabgrass. Like fights. Fights over bathrooms and black shirts and boys, cupcakes and pancakes and parts in school plays.

Of course, I have to admit, Olivia doesn't get to be in the Sisters Club, either. She doesn't get to stay up half the night laughing till she pees her pants with her two best friends in the world, who are most times right in the next bed, or the next room, or just down the hall when you need them.

Alex has this old-fashioned poster hanging in her room that's been there for as long as I can remember. The edges are all curled and it's sun-yellowed now, but it's a painting called *Two Sisters* by some guy named Bouguereau. (Joey calls him Booger-O!) He's the one who painted all those pale, sad-eyed orphan girls who look lonely. In this one, the older sister has her arms around the little one, who's holding an apple. The older sister has a blue ribbon in her hair, and dark, sad eyes, with smudges of bruise-colored roses on her cheeks.

When I was little, I used to go into Alex's room and point to that poster, and ask, "Why is she so sad? Does she miss her mom and dad?"

Alex always answered the same way: "No, she misses her sister."

"But her sister's right there," I'd say, pointing to the curly-headed cherub with the juicy green apple.

"Not that sister. The other one. The one in the middle."

I always loved Alex for that. For making me feel like there's a hole there without me. For making me feel missed.

Sisters are better in threes.

That's the truth.

The whole truth.

And nothing but the truth.

Once Upon an Earplug

I was making my famous Don't-Bug-Me-I'm-Baking cupcakes when Joey came into the kitchen, waving a moldy old copy of *Little Women* in my face. Even though the spine is cracked, the pages are yellowed, and the mustiness factor is a seven, Mom says it's not old; it's a *classic*. Joey could read it by herself, but it is (a) about as long as three Harry Potters, with teeny-tiny print; (b) full of old-fashioned kinds of words; and (c) um, well, let's just say Joey likes to ask a lot of questions. So, we've been reading it aloud together.

"Stevie, want to read *Little Women*?" Joey asked.

I held up my wooden mixing spoon dripping with chocolate peanut-butter banana cupcake batter, as if to say, "Can't you see I'm busy right now?" but Joey's face looked so eager and hopeful, I had a hard time letting her down. "Maybe while the cupcakes are baking, we can read for fifteen minutes."

"Only fifteen? How about longer?"

"That's enough to get us past the boring part."

Joey looked insulted. "Huh! There are no boring parts."

"Yah-huh. What about all that stuff about Meg and her bonnet? Admit it, Joey. Bonnets are boring."

"Says you."

Something you should know about Joey: when she gets into something, she gets *way* into it. Her latest phase: all *Little Women* all the time, bonnets or no bonnets. Case in point:

1. She gave up presents for Christmas, because in *Little Women* the dad's away at war and they don't have any money, so they have to give up Christmas presents.
2. She's started saying stuff like "I dare say! Nothing pleasant ever does happen in this family!" and "It's a dreadfully unjust world."
3. She's growing her hair to give it away to charity, so she makes me measure it a gazillion times a week!

She even wants us to call her Jo instead of Joey. I don't mind reading with her, but lately, I'd been stalling and making up excuses because we were on Chapter 38 and in two chapters is the "Valley of the Shadow," when Beth dies.

Joey is going to freak!

All of a sudden, we heard a crash from the next room, where Alex had been clickety-clacking on Dad's laptop. Joey and I went running and saw Alex teetering on the arm of the big overstuffed chair, staring in horror at Dad's laptop, which had crashed to the floor.

Good thing Dad was out in his garage/studio/workshop. He was putting in long hours building a giant genie lamp for some fat guy to pop out of in a play they're doing at the Raven Theater, next door.

"Is it broken?" Joey asked.

"Just the battery popped out, I think," Alex said, finally reaching to pick it up.

Mixing bowl and spoon in hand, I was still stirring, trying not to lose count. "Alex, Dad's going to kill you if you break that," I said.

"What's so big and important that you have to look

13

it up every five seconds, anyway?" Joey asked.

"The Drama Club at school is putting on a new play, and Mr. Cannon said they'd be announcing what it will be on the website by five o'clock today."

"It's only four thirty-three," I pointed out, still stirring counter-clockwise.

"*By* five o'clock," she said, like I'd never heard the word before. "Not *at* five o'clock. That could mean *before* five."

"Sheesh." Sometimes *sheesh* is all you can say when your sister's a DQ. Alex has taken every one of the quizzes in her teen magazines, and she always comes up DQ (Drama-not-Dairy Queen).

"What do you think it'll be?" Joey asked.

"I hope, hope, hope it's *Romeo and Juliet*," Alex said. Surprise, surprise. She's been wanting to play Juliet since the late Pleistocene era (a.k.a. 1.8 million years ago).

Alex pretended to drink poison. "'Eyes, look your last! Arms, take your last embrace ... A dateless bargain to engrossing death!'" She clutched her throat, then her stomach, then staggered and fell in a heap on the worn corduroy couch.

14

Drama Queen to the max. Alex is always pretending to faint, fall over, and die of poisoning, snakebite, stabbing, smothering, or beheading.

"I hope it's *Little Women*," said Joey. "The musical."

"You have *Little Women* on the brain," said Alex. "Besides, it's too sad, because of Beth—"

She'd been about to blow it, giving it away about Beth dying. Luckily, my hand got to her mouth just in time, so *dying* just sounded like E-I-E-I-O-ing. Never mind that I splattered chocolate peanut-butter banana batter in her hair and almost did a Cyclops on her, practically poking her eye out with my mixing spoon.

"What's too sad? What about Beth?" Joey shrieked, then covered up her ears. "No, wait, don't tell me. I don't want to know. '*Twinkle, twinkle, little star!*'" she screeched at the top of her lungs, to drown out Alex just in case.

"Sorry," Alex said when I took my hand away. I thought she'd yell at me, but instead she sucked a glob of cupcake batter from her hair. Joey saw that the coast was clear and cautiously removed her hands from her ears.

15

"It doesn't matter anyway," I told Alex. "You know the play's going to be a musical." Even though I knew how much Alex wanted the play to be a Shakespeare drama-not-comedy, I couldn't help wishing for a musical. I love musicals! It's kind of my thing to sing along when we watch them on TV, and everybody says I have a good voice.

"Nah-uh."

"Yah-huh," said Joey.

"Think about it. *High School Musical. Wicked. Dreamgirls. The Lion King. Hairspray. Legally Blonde.* Even *Young Frankenstein.* Everything's a musical."

"The Little Mermaid," Joey added.

"'Wherefore art thou'—doesn't anybody do Shakespeare anymore?" Alex said, touching the back of her hand to her forehead in a swoon.

"Not unless Shakespeare is a musical," I told her. "They even make tragedies into musicals."

"That is a tragedy," Alex said, stabbing keys on the laptop again.

"What's so bad about musicals?" Joey asked. "I love musicals. Stevie and I know tons of the songs."

"Duh!" Alex looked up. "Musicals have music, Little

16

Sister, and with music, you have to sing."

"What's wrong with that? You sing in the shower all the time."

"Yeah, but in a musical, you have to sing in front of other people. I'm an actor. Stevie's the singer in this family. I only sing where nobody but Sock Monkey can hear me."

"*I* hear you," Joey and I both said at the same time, cracking up.

"Nobody *important*," said Alex, wrinkling her nose at us.

"Fink Face!" Joey and I screamed, and we pointed at Alex, which is what we always do when Alex makes her wrinkly pug face. That face is supposed to make us mad, but really it just makes us laugh.

"Shh! Quiet, you guys. I can't think. Wait, here it is! I think this is it. Mr. Cannon must have posted it. After much discussion ... blah blah ... sure you'll be as pleased ... blah blah ... we are happy to announce ... this year's Drama Club production ... blah blah...

"*Once Upon a Mattress,* the musical!" Alex announced.

Once Upon a Time ... to buy earplugs!

Death Be Nimble,
Death Be Quick
by Joey Reel

I love to write stuff down and make lists.
I took a quiz in one of Alex's teen magazines,
and it said I was the Scribe!

Ways people die in Shakespeare that Alex is always acting out:

- Flinging themselves on top of swords or daggers
- Deadly venom of two asps (snakebite!)

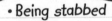

- Being stabbed
- Jumping into rivers
- Being smothered
- Being hanged

- Being poisoned
- Getting buried in sand
- Off with their heads!

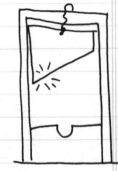

Off with Her Hair!
by Joey Reel

I started growing my hair the minute I read Chapter 15: "A Telegram." Chapter 15 in <u>Little Women</u> is the best! The March sisters find out that their dad is wounded and in the hospital, and they're poor and they don't have any money, so Jo (my favorite) chops off all her hair!!! She sells it for twenty-five dollars and gives the money to her family to help bring her dad home.

Off with her hair! ~S

So I am:

25 dollars! My hair's worth at least $250. A.

1. Growing my hair long
2. Making Stevie measure my ponytail every day
3. Waiting for it to grow to ten inches
4. Cutting off my ponytail and donating it to Locks of Love, where it will get made into a wig for kids with cancer

Hair grows SUPER slow! ~S

Best style!

WOE IS ME
Starring Alex

Me: Why did they have to pick stupid *Once Upon a Mattress*?

Sock Monkey: What's wrong with that? It's about a princess. You love playing princesses.

Me: Not dorky ones!

Sock Monkey: Whatever. A princess is a princess is a princess.

Me: Not when her name is Winnifred the Woebegone. They call her Fred.

Sock Monkey: Ha, ha, that's funny.

Me: What do you know? You're full of stuffing.

Sock Monkey: Hey, watch it.

Me: Woe is me.

Sock Monkey: Don't you mean Princess Woebegone is you?

Me: Very funny, you. This is serious! You know how long I've been wanting to act in a real play, like *Romeo and Juliet*.

Sock Monkey: People don't have to die just to make it a good play.

Me: I know. But it helps. I'm no good at comedies, anyway.

Sock Monkey: What do you mean? You're funny.

Me: Yeah, right. I think you have me mixed up with Joey. Everybody knows Joey is the Funny One in the family.

Sock Monkey: How about that time you tripped over the volcano and went flying across the stage? Everybody laughed, didn't they? That was funny.

Me: I broke my toe! That was *so* not funny.

Sock Monkey: Why don't you just try out for Lady Larken, then? She doesn't have to act silly.

Me: And let Jayden Pffeffer steal the show? I don't *think* so. If I'm going to be in the play at all, I have to at least *try* for the lead. Then if I don't get it, maybe I could still be a minor character, like Larken.

Sock Monkey: C'mon, you know you're going to try out, and you just said you're going for the lead, and you know you'll be great, so why not just admit it?

Me: I so do NOT know that.

Sock Monkey: Which?

Me: I don't know for sure that I want to go for the lead. I mean, what if I do, and I'm not great? Don't forget, it's a *musical*.

Sock Monkey: So, you'll have to sing. But it's not like you have to be a soprano like Stevie. At least the princess role is an alto. You can handle that, easy. And besides, "Happily Ever After" is really the only song you have to sing all by yourself, without anybody.

Me: A solo? That does it. I am *so* not going for the part!

Princesses and Peas
by Joey Reel

I love <u>Once Upon a Mattress</u>. Dad and I have watched it on DVD tons of times. It's like the true story of <u>The Princess and the Pea</u>. See, there's this queen, and she doesn't think any princess is good enough for the prince, so she puts twelve princesses through all these crazy, impossible tests and they never, ever pass. Then at the end they put a ton of stuff under a ton of mattresses to see if Princess Number Thirteen can feel it. If she can't sleep, she's a true princess.

Main roles in <u>Once</u> <u>Upon</u> <u>a</u> <u>Mattress</u>:

- Jester
- Minstrel
- Prince Dauntless
- Princess Winnifred the Woebegone
  (a.k.a. Fred, or Winnie)
- Queen Aggravation *You mean Queen Aggravain! A.*
- Sir Harry
- Wizard *Or is it Queen Alex-is-Vain? ~S*
- King who can't talk
- Lady Meadowlark *Hey! It's Lady Larken! A.*
- And some more Ladies-in-Waiting

She's not an Oregon state bird! ~S

Alex will want to be the princess, since that's the lead, but I think she should go for Queen because she's already bossy, so she'd just have to play herself!

Much Ado About Alex

Joey was holding a ruler up to her hair, trying to measure her own ponytail. Mom was doing research on the laptop, stressing out and making herself jealous over all the other, way-more-famous cooking shows on TV (Hello! Maybe because they actually know how to cook, whereas Mom is an actor who fakes the cooking part) and I (Yours Truly) was dreaming up highly new and original recipes for the World's Most Divine Cupcake.

Lately, I'd been baking cupcakes whenever I had stuff on my mind. Baking is a great escape—I can take everything I'm feeling and put it into making cupcakes. It's easy to lose myself in a batch of Brownie Perfection with Buttercream Frosting.

And except for the burned batch of Don't-Bug-Me cupcakes and the disgusting dozen mint ones that came out puke-colored, most of my creations are edible. I'd even been thinking about entering the First Annual Cascade County (Move-Over-Betty-Crocker) Cake-Off.

I added the Move-Over-Betty-Crocker part because bake-offs are old-school and cake-offs are way cool. Experimenting is the best part, and any that don't turn out gross (or get eaten) I squirrel away in the freezer.

The only problem was that I, Yours Truly, had to work up the courage to get Fondue Sue (i.e., Mom) and Mr. Cheapsteak (i.e., Dad) to cough up one hundred clams-smackers-greenbacks-buckaroonies-dead presidents for the entry fee.

"Hey, everybody," Alex said, sliding into the room in her sock feet. "I have an announcement."

"The Hat!" said Joey. "You have to put on The Hat if you're going to make a family announcement. It's the rules." Joey was referring to the old jester hat from *King Lear*. It's a Reel family rule that you have to wear The Hat whenever you have something big and important to say.

"No way. I am not wearing that smelly old fleabag," said Alex.

There she goes again. Always breaking the rules.

"I've been thinking—"

"That's a first," said Joey, cracking herself up. Joey never seemed to get tired of that joke.

Alex was wearing this necklace she hadn't taken off since her thirteenth birthday. It had two silver charms of the drama masks Comedy and Tragedy, kind of like good-luck charms. She nervously slid them back and forth on the chain.

"As I was saying, I've been think—I mean, I've thought it over and I've decided I'm not trying out for the play."

My heart did a double-triple, mini-somersault flip-flop inside. The happy-not-nervous kind of flip-flop, like just before you open a shiny-wrapped Christmas present. Alex NOT trying out for a play? I wasn't sure I'd heard right until everybody asked, "Why not?" at the same time.

I glanced over at Alex. Comedy seemed to be winking at me.

"C'mon, guys. It's *Once Upon a Mattress*. (a) It's stupid and (b) it's for kids."

"I'm a kid," Joey said. "And I think it's funny."

"And (c)," said Alex, ticking off the letters on her fingers, "I can't sing."

"What do you mean, you can't sing?" Dad asked. "You have a perfectly nice singing voice."

Mom stopped clacking on her keyboard and nodded in agreement.

"You know singing's not my thing. Not like Stevie."

Alex always does this. She says bad stuff about herself so people (Mom and Dad) will talk her out of it.

I, for one, was not going to talk her out of it. I was way-down-deep secretly crossing fingers, elbows, and toes, hoping Alex was *not* going to try out for the play. Because ever since I'd heard that the school play was a musical, I had the idea that I could just-might-maybe try out myself.

Alex may be the Actor in the family, but I'm the one with a good singing voice. And there are hardly any speaking lines in a musical—most of the lines you get to sing. But can I just say: if Alex found out I wanted to be in the play, she'd start acting all weird, doubting herself.

I knew Mom and Dad would tell me that if I wanted

something badly enough, I should go for it. But half the reason Alex is into acting is so she can be in the spotlight.

It's one thing for her to compete with Arch-Actress-Enemy Jayden Pffeffer. But I'm her *sister*. Even though I had as much right as she did to try out for the school play, I knew she'd think I was betraying her.

My face grew hot just thinking about trying out. I looked from my sisters to Mom and Dad. Could anybody read it on my face? Tell what I was thinking? I tried to look like maybe I was coming down with a fever.

"And (d)—" said Alex.

"And (d)," I said for her, in a sarcastic voice, "Scott Towel is not going for the part of the prince, right?" Scott Towel (real name Scott Howell, but Joey and I prefer the paper-towel version) was this kid Alex has been crushing on since the fourth grade. He happened to be the Beast in *Beauty and the Beast* when Alex played Beauty.

"Frog Lips!" said Joey (it's her other favorite name for Scott Towel). "Maybe the part isn't hairy enough for him."

"Ha, ha, very funny. FYI, I haven't talked to Scott Towel, I mean Howell. So I don't know if he's going for it or not."

"So what's your other reason, then?" Joey asked.

"Hel-lo! It's a comedy. You have to act all goofy and trip over stuff and everything."

"You're good at that!" said Joey, unfolding herself from the chair-and-a-half she'd been tucked into with a book for the last hour. She was referring to the now-famous Volcano Incident, when Alex tripped and broke her toe in *Beauty and the Beast*. At the last minute, I had stepped in to take her part since I knew all the lines. That's when I'd started to figure out that my Human Piñata days were over and maybe I could actually be in a play without dying of stage fright.

"We all remember Alex's Big Trip," Dad teased.

"Not every play has to be Shakespeare, honey," Mom said. "Musicals are wildly popular now, and they're so much fun."

I'll skip the part where Mom and Dad chatted about the Good Old Days (a.k.a. BTHK, Before They Had Kids) and reminisced about all the musicals they had been in Once Upon a Time. Major snooze.

After Dad's Big Trip (down Memory Lane) he started in on one of his famous speeches. "Mom's right, Alex. Comedy is just as valid. Shakespeare wrote comedies, too, you know. They have puns and plot twists and mistaken identities. Take *As You Like It* or *Much Ado About Nothing.* They're much more lighthearted in tone than his other works."

"Some of them even have happy endings," Mom added.

"Learning to use your body to create humor can be challenging for an actor. It's called physical comedy, and it's harder than it looks."

Dad yakked on and on about Kramer, Mr. Bean, and the Three Stooges and how they were masters of physical theater. Sometimes Dad forgets we aren't students in his classroom. He launched into explaining the pitfalls of a pratfall (i.e., landing on your butt).

How hard can it be?

"Why don't they just call it a buttfall?" I asked. Nobody heard my joke. They were too busy walking into walls, making weird faces, tossing the jester hat back and forth, and falling down on their butts, laughing. The Reel Family Clown School.

I was used to feeling left out when it came to this family and acting. Joey tumbled off the couch. OK, so acting has never been my thing, but if that's acting, I can fall on my butt as well as the next person.

"Watch this," I called, joining in. I held the back of my hand to my head in a fake faint, took three steps backwards, stumbled over the "half" part of the chair-and-a-half and crumpled to the floor, landing on my butt, legs in the air. Joey pointed and laughed the hardest.

Acting, I thought, catching my breath. *How hard can it be?* But if I tried out for an actual play, would I fall on my butt for real?

Everybody knew Alex was the Actor-with-a-Capital-A. The Pretty One. Just like Joey was the Smart One and the Funny One. And I was the Sensible One. Calm. Even-tempered. Levelheaded. We each had parts to play, even in our own family. I felt like I was breaking a major rule just by *thinking* about acting in a play. Like when I crossed the line of tape into Alex's room—the one we weren't supposed to step over without her permission.

YOU are a STAR!

Whether it's in the spotlight or behind the scenes, find out what role in a play fits you best.

- -

1. You have opening-night jitters. To relax, you decide to . . .

a. Sit quietly, breathe, and picture the ocean in your mind.

b. Yell at your sister.

c. Rub your tummy, pat your head, and chew gum at the same time.

d. Park yourself in the back row and refuse to get up onstage no matter what.

2. It's opening night, and Romeo has just tripped over Juliet's dress and fallen flat on his face. Do you . . . ?

a. Keep acting, even in your underwear.

b. Yell out, "The show must go on!"

c. Quick! Drop the curtain!

d. Laugh your pants off and give them a standing ovation.

continued on next page →

QUIZ

3. What do you most look for in a good play?

a. Makes you want to sing and dance along.

b. Makes you think.

c. Makes you get so wrapped up you forget if the lights are working.

d. Makes you laugh.

4. Cast party! You are the host. What would you like your invitations to say?

a. Come celebrate me, me, me!

b. Be there or else!

c. B.Y.O.P. Bring your own paintbrush and let's create!

d. Don't miss: instant video replays of bloopers.

5. The first review of your play has just hit the blogosphere. What do you hope it says?

a. The lead actor stole the show!

b. Brilliant interpretation of a classic tale.

c. The play was saved by outstanding set design and costumes.

d. Thunderous applause brought down the house.

6. At last the play is over, and it's time to unwind at the beach. Would you . . . ?

a. Sing to the seagulls.

b. Organize a beach volleyball game.

c. Build an elaborate sand castle.

d. Kick back on your beach towel and people-watch.

If you chose mostly a's, you're an:

★ **ACTOR/SUPERSTAR**

- You're a people person and enjoy the company of others.
- You like to be in the spotlight, with all eyes on you.
- There's no sound greater than the roar of applause.

If you chose mostly b's, you're a:

★ **DIRECTOR**

- You're the boss!
- You love to give orders and be in charge.
- You are highly organized and see the big picture.

If you chose mostly c's, you're a:

★ **CREW MEMBER/COSTUME DESIGNER**

- You're a hands-on, behind-the-scenes person.
- You love to build, paint, and create.
- You are multi-talented and able to multitask.

If you chose mostly d's, you're an:

★ **AUDIENCE MEMBER**

- You love to laugh, cry, and be entertained.
- Nothing beats sitting in the dark and getting swept up in a good story.
- Your friends look to you for feedback and support.

Cupcake Maths
by Joey Reel

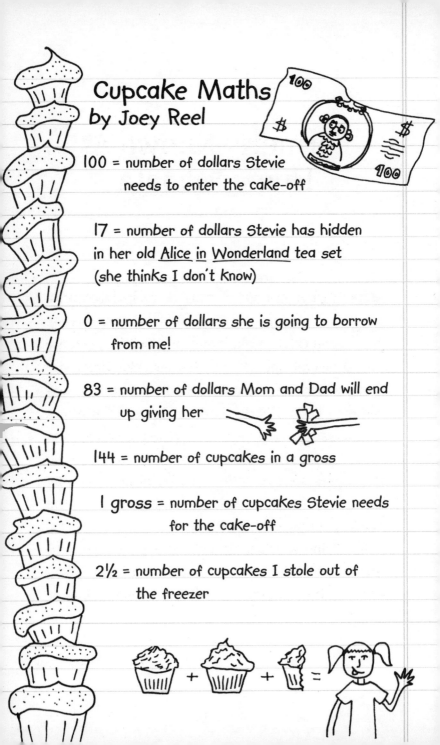

100 = number of dollars Stevie needs to enter the cake-off

17 = number of dollars Stevie has hidden in her old <u>Alice in Wonderland</u> tea set (she thinks I don't know)

0 = number of dollars she is going to borrow from me!

83 = number of dollars Mom and Dad will end up giving her

144 = number of cupcakes in a gross

1 gross = number of cupcakes Stevie needs for the cake-off

2½ = number of cupcakes I stole out of the freezer

Formerly Known as Human Piñata

So, I had a secret. I had decided—I was going to try out for the play. And I was dying to tell Best Friend Olivia, even though it wasn't the gossipy kind of secret she always tells me, like when you know something about somebody you're not supposed to know. The kind Olivia always knew about kids at school or people on her street. Olivia lives in a tree-lined, ride-your-bike neighborhood, where all the houses are thirty-three shades of beige and fly flags with pumpkins and hearts and snowmen at the exact right time of year.

According to Olivia, there's always somebody to spy on, which I guess you would do a lot of if you were an Only and didn't have any sisters to bug or hang out with. There was the time Olivia saw a stolen lawn gnome from Mrs. Jaszczak's front yard in a seventh grader's locker at school, and the time she heard Sean Vandemeer's dad yelling his head off when he found out that Sean had driven the car even though he was only fourteen.

We Reels live in Acton's oldest house, a run-down Victorian right off Main Street that is as shaggy as a eucalyptus tree from all the peeling paint on the outside. Mom likes to joke that the termites have eaten all the fancy gingerbread trim around the roof and porch.

Our neighbors are the Raven Theater, which my family owns; the fire department; and an empty lot that used to be a Christmas-tree farm in the way-old days until a Scurry of Pocket Gophers decided to use it as their home address.

"Look on the bright side," I told Mom and Dad the other day when they were remembering the Christmas-tree farm and lamenting. "At least it wasn't taken over by an Implausibility of Gnus."

This, by the way, is what you'd call Applied Learning. We were studying animal group names (a Glint of

Goldfish, a Quiver of Cobras) in school, and I *applied* what I was *learning*. Kind of like using a vocabulary word in a sentence.

Hint: it's always a good idea to show off What You Are Learning at School right before hitting your parents for a hundred big ones.

It was hard to concentrate on schoolwork or cupcakes, though, because all I could think about was the musical. At first it was just an idea. A wish. A possibility. My pulse raced just thinking about it.

Then it started to grow, taking up more and more space in me. No matter how much I tried to brush it away, I just couldn't swat it dead like it was one of a Business of Flies or something. Pretty soon I was thinking about it while I was reading *Little Women* to Joey or watching reruns of Mom's cooking show on basic cable or making Cavalcades of Cupcakes (I made that one up!) for the Cascade County Cake-Off.

That once-tiny pulse had turned into heart thumping excitement. Me! In a play! Singing my heart out. Onstage. But I couldn't breathe a word of it to anyone.

Why the big secret?

Well, when you happen to have a big sister who's good at everything and is the Actress in the family, and when you've had stage fright ever since your first acting role as a Human Piñata, and when you have always been the one in the family who hates acting, and when you've spent eleven and a half years trying to be good at other stuff even though you finally got to stand in for your sister in *Beauty and the Beast* because she broke her toe and you knew all the lines and you realized your stage fright was all in your head and that standing in that small spot of light in a room full of breathless dark with everybody holding their breath because of you, YOU ... well, then it was kind of hard to admit that you even wanted to act in a play.

To get up onstage. To sing.

In fact, it was absolutely positively terrifying, especially because Alex is, was, and always would be the Princess. Oldest sister. Snow White. Dorothy. Beauty. And if Alex was the Princess in the family, what did that make me?

The Pea.

I am the pea.

* * *

I finally called Olivia to tell her for real. Since this was only the Biggest Secret of My Life, I took the cordless phone down into the basement and hid behind the gurgling water heater, whispering the whole time just in case.

For the rest of the week, every time I caught myself getting excited about the play, I tried to shrink my secret down to pea size. *Don't get your hopes up too high,* I warned myself.

But a little voice inside me would not be quiet. What if I got to stand in the spotlight for once, the way I had for one shining moment in *Beauty*? What if I wasn't the pea? What if the princess was me?

What if, what if, what if … ? In no time, my excitement had suddenly double-triple-quadrupled until I was staring at a secret the size of a Pandemonium of Parrots.

So I pretended not to have a secret. Pretending was kind of like acting, which was kind of like practicing for an audition without anybody knowing.

How did this happen? Me. The Pea. I was supposed to be the Practical One. Instead, it felt like that first

41

time I'd jumped off the high dive when I was seven. Reckless and brave ... and exciting.

The part I hated to imagine was telling my family my secret. I tried not to picture Mom and Dad looking at me like I was a Benedict-Arnold-size traitor and Joey gaping like I'd gone stark-raving, Jane-Eyre mad and Alex running from the room, stung, the same as if I'd just slapped her fresh across the face.

Weird and Cool-Sounding Names for Groups of Animals
by Joey Reel
(copied from Stevie's science notebook!)

- A Sleuth of Bears
- A Flutter of Butterflies
- A Nuisance of Cats
- An Intrusion of Cockroaches
- A Murder of Crows
- A Memory of Elephants
- A Business of Flies
- An Implausibility of Gnus
- A Charm of Hummingbirds
- A Smack of Jellyfish
- A Lounge of Lizards
- A Carload of Monkeys
- A Raft of Otters
- A Pandemonium of Parrots
- A Prickle of Porcupines

An Arrogance of Actors ~S
A Choir of Copycats A.
A Conceit of Cuckoos ~S

Seven Ways Stevie Is Acting Super-Strange
by Joey Reel

1. Madly baking My-Sister-Is-a-Drama-Queen cupcakes. This can only mean one thing: something is bugging her (Alex)

2. Singing musical scales night and day (not just the normal Beatles songs in the shower)

3. Crossing the line of duct tape into Alex's room, tearing through her closet, and trying on her black shirt

4. Practicing walking with a book on her head!

5. Staggering around in Alex's Mom-Didn't-Want-to-Buy-Me-Eighth-Grade-School-Dance high heels and falling down all over the place

6. Pretending to faint and fall back on her bed, over and over

7. Not even mad that twenty-seven stuffed animals are acting out an Operatic Tragedy from <u>Little Women</u> all over her side of the room

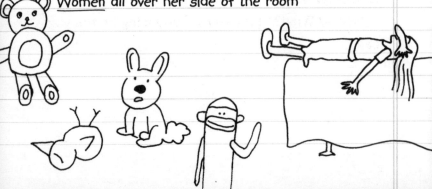

Super Sister Secret

"What's up with you?" Joey asked me in our room that evening, sitting on a giant green bouncy yoga ball.

"What do you mean? Nothing's up," I told her. But my insides were screaming, *I've decided to try out for a part in the musical!*

"Yah-huh. You're acting weird."

"Am not."

"Yah-huh. I have proof." Joey handed over her notebook with a list of seven ways I'm acting strange.

"OK, Joey. But you can't tell. Not anybody. Especially Alex."

"What? What?" Joey started bouncing on the yoga ball.

"Listen to me. This is a big-time Super Sister Secret. You have to triple-cross-your-heart-hope-to-die, quadruple-zip-your-lips promise you won't tell."

"I promise. This is so great." Joey clutched her hands to her heart. "Now I'll know a secret. Like how Jo, when she meets Laurie, is sure he has a dark secret. A *tragic European* secret."

"OK, but if you tell ..." *Snip, snip, snip.* I made scissors with my fingers, threatening to cut off her ponytail.

"Blast and wretch," said Joey, reaching to protect her ponytail.

I cleared my throat. I coughed. I sputtered. "Guess what? I'm going to try out for the play."

"You? What play? Not—"

"Once Upon a Mattress," I finished the sentence for her.

Joey stopped bouncing. Her face morphed from uncertainty to recognition to horror.

"Alex's play?" she breathed.

I nodded. "Except it's not Alex's play, because she's not trying out, remember?"

"Wow, you'll be the best Princess Winnie ever!" Joey said, spinning around the room.

I blushed. "Joey, that's the lead. I can't go for *the lead*."

"Why not? Sure you can. Your voice is perfect, and you already know all the songs. This is so great. I can just picture you singing 'Happily Ever After.'"

Joey was saying out loud what I had already been secretly thinking and imagining to myself. "Well … maybe I could. Maybe I should. Do you really think so?"

Joey bobbed her head up and down, still flinging herself around the room, humming "Happily Ever After."

I took a deep breath. The fact that Joey thought I should try out for Winnie felt like a sign. "OK, I'll do it. I'll try out — for the lead. But you still can't tell. Not till I'm ready."

Joey pretended to zip up her lips. "This is big!" she cried. "This is so big! No wonder you've been acting so really weird!"

HOW DO YOU SOLVE A PROBLEM LIKE ALEX?
Starring Alex

Me: *(Entering Stevie and Joey's room, hearing them talking.)* What's big?

Stevie and Joey: *(At same time.)* Nothing!

Me: Then how come you look so guilty? I can always tell when you guys are keeping a secret, so you might as well just tell me.

Joey: *(Rearranges stuffed animals on her bed.)* Stevie didn't go in your room, honest! And she definitely didn't go in your closet.

Stevie: *(Makes mad eyes at Joey.)* Joey!

Me: I didn't say you guys were in my room. Were you?

Joey: Never mind. That's not the real secret, anyway.

Stevie: *(Throws pillow at Joey.)* Jo-ey!

Joey: Hey, no throwing pillows. It's against Sisters Club rules.

Me: Ha! *(Points at Joey.)* So, my dear Watson,

we've established that there is, in fact,
a secret.

Joey: A Super Sister Secret!

Stevie: Joey, a pox on you if you breathe
one word!

Me: It's OK. You can tell me, Duck. I'm your
sister. Was Stevie in my closet, trying on
my heels? Is that it?

Joey: *(Imitating* Little Women.*)* "What
cunning little heels! You have to have
heels!"

Me: Jo-ey?

Joey: She wasn't *not* in your closet.

Me: Precisely, Watson. Just as I thought.

Stevie: *(Biting on end of hair.)* Enough
about secrets! Didn't you have something
you wanted to tell us?

Joey: I know—why don't we make this a
Sisters Club Meeting?

Stevie: Yeah!

Joey: *(Holding up stuffed animal
hedgehog.)* Hedgie can be our mascot,
instead of Sock Monkey.

Me: OK. Sisters, Blisters, and Tongue
Twisters. Official meeting of the Sisters
Club, now in session.

Joey: Hey, we didn't hook pinkies!

Everybody: *(Hooking pinkies.)* Sisters,
Blisters, and Tongue Twisters.

Joey: This is so cool! It's just like the
Pickwick Club—that's the secret society
Jo and her sisters have in *Little Women.*
I could be Augustus Snodgrass and
Stevie—

Me: Pickwick Club! Might as well call it the
Pick-Your-Nose Club.

Joey: C'mon, you guys. Let's bare our souls
and tell the most appalling secrets, like
they do in the Pickwick Club.

Me: *(Wrinkling nose.)* Whatever. Look, we
have to go with Dad to pick up Mom
from work. They're taking us to House
of Cheese for pizza, so we don't have
much time.

Joey: Yum!

Stevie: So what's up?

Me: Well, I have some exciting news.
I've been thinking about it for a while,
and I've decided ... Are you ready for
this?... I'm going to try out for the play
after all. I've decided just to go
for it, so I'm going to go out for the
lead in *Once Upon a Mattress.*

Joey: *(Looks at Stevie, mouth open.)*

Stevie: *(Looks at Joey, turns beet red.)*

Joey: The lead? Did you say the lead?

Me: Sure. Why not? Why are you acting so
weird?

Joey: You mean the princess?

Me: Yes, the princess. Of course, the
princess. What else *but* the princess?

Joey: But what about—what about how you
hate musicals?

Stevie: And what about how you can't sing?

Me: Thanks a lot!

Joey: In front of people, she means.

Me: So I'll take a few voice lessons. The music
teacher at school might help me or something. What do you think? Isn't it exciting?

Stevie: Yeah, thrilling.

Joey: That's—that's—that's ... great.

Me: What's wrong? I thought this would be big giant news.

Stevie: *(Sarcastically.)* News flash! Alex Reel is going to star in yet another play for like the one-millionth time!

Me: *(Standing in doorway, about to leave.)* Well, you don't have to act so snot-faced about it. Geez! You're my sisters. I thought you'd at least be happy for me. And you guys wonder why sometimes I don't want to be in the Sisters Club.

Dad: *(Calls upstairs.)* Time to go and pick up Mom!

Joey: Wait! Don't go yet. The meeting's not over. Stevie has something she wants to tell you. Don't you, Stevie?

Stevie: Um, yeah. Good luck.

The Sisters Club
by Joey Reel

0 = number of Sisters Club Meetings
     lately, till today

1 = number of sisters who want to change name to
     Pickwick Club

0 = number of sisters who want to change name
     to Pick-Your-Nose Club

eww! A.

1 = number of times Hedgie got
     to be mascot

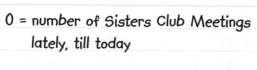

5 = number of times Stevie really tried on
     Alex's heels

2 = number of sisters who BOTH want to try out
     for the lead in the play!

MINE!   **Script**   NO
                        MINE!

The Tempest

On the way to Mom's studio, I let it sink in that Alex was going to try out for the play. Really and truly. My excitement over trying out myself had gone out of me, like air out of a day-after party balloon.

What goes up must come down.

I stared out the window. Fog. Gray January fog. No mountains in sight. Usually the snowcapped peaks of the Three Sisters, like frosted cupcakes, were silhouetted against the purple-streaked sky. No drama in the skies today, just inside me.

We get three kinds of gray skies in Oregon: white-gray, light-gray, and gray-gray, and today was gray-gray. I could imagine Joey spouting *Little Women:* "'There is always light behind the clouds.'"

Not today.

Now the fog had gone to twilight, which was turning to night.

The backseat was quiet. Not the dreamy kind of quiet when you stare lazily out the window and all's right with the world. The frozen quiet like a wall between two sisters that feels hard as ice.

Alex kept stealing sideways glances at me. She looked nervous, like I was a shaken-up bottle of pop about to explode. But as soon as our eyes met, she quickly looked out the window.

Good thing Joey was smushed in between Alex and me. For once, I wasn't in the middle. But I was in the middle of a giant mess.

Why did Alex have to decide to be in the play, anyway? She didn't even like musicals. Or singing in front of people. Why couldn't she, just once, be the audience, not the actor?

Dad was listening to news on the radio. The annoying radio guy was droning on and on, buzzing like a Scourge of Mosquitoes.

"Dad! Could you turn that thing down?" I said, louder than I meant to. "Please," I added, a little softer.

I felt like I was in a mixing bowl myself—all churned up. Why did Alex have to go for the lead? How could I even be thinking of trying out for the same role as Alex? She was the oldest. The Pretty One. The Actress. The *Princess*. How could I compete with that? How could I compete with my own *sister*?

Anger sizzled inside me like hot oil in a pan, just thinking about it. Maybe I should just forget the whole thing. Drop it. Chalk it up to Stupid Idea Number 297.

But a little voice inside me wouldn't quit. I love to sing, and finally the school was putting on a musical. Why shouldn't I make my voice heard?

I was still seething when we pulled up outside the ugly brownish-beige box that is Mom's building.

"I'll tell Mom we're here," I said, fleeing the confines of the car.

"I'll go with you," Alex said, and flip-flopped after me without a coat, even though it was freezing out.

At the front desk, we signed in and grabbed badges that said *V* for Visitor. I headed down the hall, past offices and sound booths with glass windows; past bulletin boards with notices of the county cake-off tempting me; to the studio, where they taped the *Fondue Sue* show.

The door was closed, but we could see through the large glass window. It was mostly black, with tons of cords and wires and boxes with dials everywhere. The light was on in Mom's kitchen set.

"They're still in there," said Alex.

"We can't go in yet," I replied flatly. "The red ON AIR light's still lit." I pointed to the panel above the door.

Alex kept glancing at me as I thumbed through some magazine article about the plight of the polar bear, snapping the slick pages so hard I ripped one.

Glaciers could move, polar ice caps could melt, but there would be no moving my sister. No changing her mind.

"I don't get you, Stevie," said Alex. "Why are you so mad at me? You weren't even the least bit happy for me when I decided to try out for the play—"

"Yeah, like you ever *weren't* trying out for the play," I said in a snotty voice.

Alex looked hurt. "What do you mean?"

"You know exactly what I mean. All that stuff about *It's a stupid musical* and *Ooh, I can't sing!*" I said sarcastically. "You knew all along you were going to try out for it. So don't pretend like you didn't."

I knew I was being bratty, but I couldn't help what I was feeling. Anger. Frustration. Resentment.

There are no rules for feelings.

"OK, first of all, stop yelling. They'll hear you in there. Second of all, since when do you care if I do or don't try out for a play? You hate acting. You're the one person in our family who doesn't give a flying burrito about any of this stuff."

"Ha! You think you're the only one ... never mind." I stared a hole through the polar bear in the magazine. One polar bear became two, four, six as my eyes blurred with hot tears. I tried my hardest not to think of things that would make me cry.

"Wait a minute," Alex said, pointing an accusing finger at me. "Hold everything. You ... you want to ... *you're* going to try out for *my* play!"

That's when I lost it. I flew into a rage. All I wanted to do was reach over and rip out a giant hunk of her dark, curly hair.

"Yes, OK? So you know my secret. I'm trying out for the play!" My voice rose. "That's right. The same play. The lead. Same as you." I had started out shrill, but now I was practically screaming. "Why do I always have to be the one who hates acting? I like plays as much as anybody! I was good that time I had to be Beauty for you. And you said you weren't trying out—" My voice cracked, and I started to hiccup. "Why'd you have to go and ruin everything?"

"Me? Ruin everything? Look who's talking!" I stepped back, but Alex just moved closer. "How dare you! All this time I've been talking about the play, and you go and stab me in the back. My own sister."

The studio door flew open. "Girls!" Mom said sharply. "Alex. Stevie. What on earth—"

"Mom, sorry, I was trying to talk to Stevie and she just went off on me—"

"I don't want to hear it," Mom said angrily. "This is my place of work." She lowered her voice. "I'm on thin ice around here as it is. You can't just come in here and start screaming in the hall. I can hear you in the soundproof studio, for goodness' sake."

"Mom, I can explain," I started.

"Where's Dad?" she demanded.

"In the car with Joey."

She pointed down the hall to the front door. "Outside. In the car. Both of you. This instant."

BITTEN BY THE BUG
Starring Alex

Me: Stevie is such a fink.

Sock Monkey: You're just upset because
she's trying out for the play.

Me: All of a sudden, just like that, out
of the blue, she wants to act in plays.
I don't get her.

Sock Monkey: Maybe she's been bitten by the
bug. Like you.

Me: But acting is MY thing. You know she's
just doing this to spite me. I mean,
if she's going to do it, why go for
the lead?

Sock Monkey: So you're mad you might have
to share the limelight?

Me: Of course I'm mad. She's my sister.
I have enough competition with girls
who aren't in my own family.

Sock Monkey: What's so bad about Stevie
sharing some of the spotlight?

Me: Have you heard that girl sing? Her
voice is ten times better than mine.

She can sing *do-re-mi* and it makes you feel all gooey inside. Even if the song is some stupid oldie from the radio, to hear her sing it, it breaks your heart and makes you want to cry.

Sock Monkey: Don't you think you're exaggerating?

Me: Ha! I can hear her practicing scales and stuff when she goes down into the basement. She thinks nobody can hear, but her voice comes straight up through the heating vent.

Sock Monkey: If you open the vent all the way, put your ear up against it, and listen really hard, you mean.

Me: Well, yeah!

Sock Monkey: So you're afraid she'll get the lead, because she's so good at singing?

Me: Duh! What have I been saying? Have you even been listening to a word I've said?

Sock Monkey: Sorry. Just asking. Well, she may be really good at singing, but you're really good at acting, right? So, do your best. You have the acting thing down, now

you just have to work on your singing.
Practice a lot and stuff.

Me: You're right. I'll just have to work
really hard at it. Come to think of it,
I did see a sign up at school about a
voice coach. Maybe I could get him to
help me, give me some tips.

Sock Monkey: That's a great idea! But even
if you work really hard and do a good job,
would it be so bad if Stevie got the lead?

Me: Yes!

Sock Monkey: Because she's your little
sister and she beat you at something?
Because it means you don't win? Or because
you think you won't be special anymore?

Me: *(Quiet.)* No comment.

Sock Monkey: Remember: you'll always be
you. Nobody can take that away.

Me: How'd you get so smart?

Sock Monkey: Hanging around you, I guess.

Me: You must be a firstborn in your sock
monkey family.

Sock Monkey: I guess that's it!

Who's the Maddest of Them All?
by Joey Reel

- STEVIE: Mad at Alex because she said she wasn't trying out for the play, then changed her mind
- ALEX: Mad at Stevie for wanting to try out for the same role in the same play
- MOM: Double mad: (1) mad at Stevie and Alex for yelling in the hall at her workplace and (2) mad that they might cancel her Fondue Sue show
- DAD: Mad that Stevie and Alex didn't come to him to talk and blew up while at Mom's workplace instead

I'm the only one who's not mad at all.
Hey, wait! I am mad.

- JOEY: Mad that everybody being mad ruined our whole pizza dinner at the House of Cheese

The Perfect Storm

The next day, Alex and I stayed mad at each other. It was all I could think about the whole day at school. By the time I got home, I was bouncing off the walls. I had to do something. Anything to quiet the emotions ping-ponging inside me. Run around the block? Maybe. Yell at Alex some more? What good would that do?

There was only one thing I could think of doing. One thing that always calmed me down. Not because it took my mind off things, but because I could put all my feelings into it.

Cupcakes.

I like making cupcakes way more than eating them. I love dreaming up new ones—not just the ingredients and recipes, but names for them that match the way I'm feeling in the moment. I even like measuring stuff—it gives an order to things that feel jumbled in my head. Beating the eggs and mixing the batter is the best part—a great outlet for when I am mad at Alex.

I thumbed through the chocolate-fingerprinted dessert cookbook. Aha! Flour, sugar, butter, cocoa, milk, vanilla, eggs. The perfect recipe for a perfect batch of I-Hate-My-Sister cupcakes. Devil's food cupcakes with dark chocolate buttercream frosting. A classic.

I measured everything but the eggs into a bowl and started mixing. I beat and beat the buttery mixture by hand, stirring and whipping the fluffy batter into a frenzy. Who needed an electric mixer when my own arm was a buzz saw of swirling and whirling motion?

Just as I was finishing up beating my cake batter into a tornado, the phone rang. It was Olivia. I stretched the not-cordless phone on the kitchen wall over to the counter so I could fold in the eggs. Next I started scooping batter into muffin tins.

"So, you're really and truly going for it, huh?" Olivia asked. "Princess Winnifred, I mean."

"Why shouldn't I? Give me one good reason—"

"Alex."

"I know, but, it just bugs me, I guess. I mean, all this time, I've been too afraid to get up onstage, then I finally do it as a favor to Alex and everything, and now it's like she's mad that I might like acting."

"What a Fink Face."

"When I wasn't into acting, all she did was bug me about how great it is to be in plays and how I didn't understand anything and how I was like a traitor to my own family because they're all into acting."

"I guess she's just worried," said Olivia.

"But why?"

"You know. She wants to be the only one good at it. And now you come along …"

"I guess. But who says I'm even any good? Maybe I stink."

"You didn't stink in *Beauty*."

"Yeah, but that was only one scene."

"You're great at singing. Maybe she's just scared that you'll steal the one thing she's good at, you know, like the thing that's hers."

"But I've spent my whole life always doing the opposite of Alex on purpose. I mean, where's the rule that says I'm not allowed to like acting? Maybe I only said all that stuff about hating it because it was always Alex's thing, and I wanted to find my own thing. Be my own person. I don't see why just once I can't forget about Alex and do something I'd really like to do."

"See? You said it yourself. It's like you've broken a rule. A Reel rule."

"A real rule? As opposed to a fake rule?"

"No, a *Reel* rule. As in a Reel family rule."

Alex was the Actor in our family. Joey was the Reader, and Writer. And I was … what? The Singer? The Good Cook? End of story?

More to the point, I was the Peacemaker. My role had always been to keep the peace, and suddenly I was doing just the opposite—stirring things up.

Like some freak of nature, I had upset the balance.

"But do you think I'm crazy to be doing this? I mean, I'm fine with the singing, but the thought of acting still makes me feel like throwing up. And don't forget, it means competing against Alex and everything."

"You know what I always say."

"Never watch a scary movie alone?"

"Not that. Some rules are made to be broken."

Louisa May Alcott's Pen Names
by Joey Reel

- Aunt Weedy
- A. M. Barnard
- Oranthy Bluggage
- Minerva Moody
- Tribulation Periwinkle
- Flora Fairfield

Possible pen names for Joey Reel:
- Josephine Oregon
- JoJo Manx
- Joseph Pinkerton ⟶
- JoAnn Justify
- JoAmy Megbeth
- Jezebel Jones

How about Zoey Peel? ~S

Eliza Inkwell! A.

I.M. Notetaker (ha ha) ~S

I got it! Penny Pencilpincher! A.

Hey! Quit messing up my list. I need an eraser. —J

That's it! You should be Anita Eraser (grin grin) ~S

The Greatest-Ever
Little Women Fake-Out

While the cupcakes were cooling, Joey came to me, making hound-dog eyes and puppy-dog paws, begging me to read *Little Women*.

"Later."

"That's what you always say. Never mind. I'll just read it myself."

Joey clomped up the stairs before I could stop her. In twelve seconds flat, she was back in the kitchen. "It's gone!" she said, pointing upstairs. "*Little Women*. It's not on the shelf over my bed, where I always keep it."

I'd known all along I couldn't put off reading Chapter 40 forever, so I was prepared. "Never mind, Duck. I just happened to see a different copy of *Little Women* at my school library, and I checked it out for us. It was supposed to be a surprise."

"But where's … I mean, what about the one we were reading?"

"Just go upstairs and get my backpack," I said, sounding as bossy as Alex.

Joey shrugged and trudged upstairs, then came trudging back down, dragging the backpack behind her. "This thing weighs ten tons," she said, handing it over.

"Can I help it if they give us ten tons of homework?" I dug through my pack and wrestled the library book out of the bag.

"Ta-da!" I half sang, trying to make it sound like a whoop-de-do big deal. "Here's the one I found at the library. It's a much cooler version of *Little Women*. See? It's not all musty-old like the one we've been reading."

"But I like the one we've been reading. It was Mom's copy when she was a girl. And before that, it was Gram's. It's like a tradition."

"Yeah, but we don't even know where that one is, so how about we start a new tradition? This can be like our own *Little Women*. Yours and mine."

"I don't know. It doesn't look right."

"They just made the print bigger so it's easier to read. See? I'll be able to read way faster now." I opened the book at a random page. "'What do you hate most?' asked Fred. 'Spiders and rice pudding.' 'What do you like best?' asked Jo. 'Dancing and French gloves,'" I said, reading super-fast.

"But look at Jo. That doesn't even look like her. She doesn't wear a pink dress like that, and her hair is darker."

"Joey. It's just a drawing. Jo looks however you want her to look—in your imagination."

"Well, it doesn't even look long enough. What if they've cut something out and I miss a part? I don't want to miss anything. It says 'abridged edition.' What does *abridged* mean, anyway?"

Sheesh. I hadn't counted on Joey being Little Miss Picky. "I think it just means they added notes to help explain stuff," I said, trying my best to convince her. "Like a bridge, to help you with hard words, you know, stuff like that." Before Joey could protest any more, I started to read:

"The pleasantest room in the house was set apart for Beth, and in it was gathered everything that she most loved— flowers, pictures, her piano…"

71

The chapter went quickly, probably because I was nervous and reading so fast. Or maybe it was the abridged thing. Every time I glanced up at Joey, she was hanging on every word of the story, hugging Hedgie to her. Luckily, she seemed to have forgotten all about the other *Little Women*. The real one, where Beth kicks the bucket. In this one, they skip the part where Beth quietly draws her last breath in the dark hour before dawn and all that.

When I was finished, Joey sat back quietly, without saying a word.

Phew. My switcheroo of the *Little Women* books had actually worked. I hadn't been sure I could fake Joey out, but she didn't even seem to suspect that anything was wrong. "Did you like that chapter?" I asked.

Joey nodded. She did not even beg me for one more chapter, like she always did.

The Real, True, and Loyal Not-Abridged Chapter 40
by Joey Reel

POOF

Stevie thinks she's so smart. But I knew <u>Little Women</u> didn't just go poof (!) and vanish into thin air all by itself. So I started looking.

That's when I found the Trail of Crumbs. Hansel and Gretel couldn't have done it better. I followed the cereal crumbs until I figured out where she'd hidden the real book — in the empty box of raisin bran on the top shelf where I can't reach. Hello! Didn't my sister ever hear of a chair?

Five things missing in Stevie's <u>Little</u> <u>Women</u> book:

1. Chapter 40 is called "Valley of the Shadow."
2. Stevie left out the whole first paragraph, where it says "the inevitable" (dictionary definition = "certain to happen"!).
3. She didn't even read Jo's poem "My Beth."
4. In the real book, even the birds say good-bye to Beth.
5. She never said <u>last</u> breath!

RAISIN BRAN

Reel v. Reel

I was in the kitchen frosting cupcakes when Mom got home. "Hmm. Looks like another Reel Family Kitchen Cupcake Invasion," Mom joked.

"Taste," I said, handing over a bite.

"Mmm, good," she said, licking her fingers. "You should make these for the cake-off." A good sign. I have to admit making cupcakes was a bit of a bribe, hoping maybe she'd forgotten about me going banshee at her place of work.

"Where's Dad?" she asked. I tilted my head towards the next room, where he was watching the news. Mom went into the family room to find Dad.

I could hear them talking in low voices. I leaned my head out of the kitchen and listened at the doorway.

"Alex has to realize …" "But Stevie just wants to …" They were talking about Alex and me.

Alex shuffled into the kitchen, wearing her fuzzy Uggs over her flannel pajama pants. "What are they saying?"

"She speaks!" I said. When Alex is mad, she never talks to me when we're alone in a room.

My sister looked at me like I was weird. "What are these?" she asked, leaning in to take a whiff of my cupcakes.

"Just a batch of I-Hate-My—um, I mean, just cupcakes. Devil's food."

"So, how mad are they?" Alex asked, nodding towards the family room.

"On a scale of We Didn't Do Our Homework to We Burned Down the House, I'd say halfway in between."

"Are we in trouble?" Alex asked.

"I don't know yet. I wish some people would just turn off the TV to make it easier on us eavesdroppers," I said.

"I know," Alex agreed, taking a swipe of frosting right off the top of a perfectly iced cupcake.

"Hey!" I said, swatting her hand, and for a second it was just like nothing had happened between us.

"They're still talking about us, you know," she reported.

"I know."

"We're going to have to face the music."

"I know."

"Any minute they're going to put on The Hat and start making an announcement or call a family meeting or something."

"I know."

"Let's be the ones to go in there first."

"Good idea. Maybe we'll get points for going to them for once, instead of them coming to us."

Alex smiled at me to distract me from her taking another swipe of icing. She headed into the family room. I followed her.

"Kids," Mom started. "About last night at the studio, we didn't get a chance to talk—"

"We know, Mom," I said.

"And we've already said we're sorry," said Alex, not sounding very sorry. I shot her a don't-make-it-worse glance.

"Look, girls," said Mom. "We know you're sorry, but you have to promise us that this kind of thing isn't going to happen again."

"Especially not at Mom's place of work," said Dad, the worry lines deepening in his forehead. "She's got enough to deal with at the studio already."

Mom massaged her forehead as if she were trying to smooth out her own worry lines. "I just wanted to say, I know I didn't handle the situation in the best way. But I'd had a long day, and the station manager was on at me because our ratings are down."

"Are they really thinking of canceling the show?" Alex asked, licking the last traces of chocolate from her finger.

"Cool," said Joey, coming downstairs. "Then we'd be poor like Jo in *Little Women*."

"Joey, get a clue," said Alex.

"Never mind that now," said Mom. "As I was saying, I know I haven't been available much lately, and I know I expect a lot from you kids, but I need to know that you girls are not going to be at each other's throats night and day over this play. Stevie, I want you to apologize to Alex. And, Alex, if Stevie is serious about trying out for this play, I want you to support her, or to at least let us know that you're OK with her decision."

"OK, I am sorry, Alex," I admitted. "I mean, I didn't mean to yell or get us in a fight. But I think I have just as much right as you to be in the play."

"I guess," said Alex.

"And Stevie, I need you to think hard about your decision. Are you really serious about trying out for this play? Have you thought about what it means? Because if you're going to try out for the lead, I don't have to tell you, it's a big commitment."

"There's more than one part in a play, you know," Dad pointed out.

I stood with one leg crossed over the other, braiding and unbraiding a chunk of hair. "I know, I know. Look, if anybody knows, I do. I've watched Alex and everybody go through it like a million and one times."

"And what about the big cake-off?" Mom added. "Have you thought about that?"

Alex butted in. "Mom, if she gets a big part in the play, she's not going to have time for both. Trust me.

Mr. Cannon is a bear when it comes to showing up for play practice."

"I thought we didn't have the money, with Mom's show in trouble and everything. For the cake-off, I mean. It costs a hundred dollars just to enter."

"You have some of your own money, kiddo," said Dad.

"And maybe you can get some pet-sitting money, and ask Gram and Grandpa," Mom said.

"Just do your best, Stevie. Mom and I will take care of the rest."

"Now, you all know, Dad's got a lot of work on the *Aladdin* sets—" Mom started.

"He's got to make a giant magic carpet fly!" said Joey.

"What Mom's saying is," Dad continued, "I'm going to be putting in long hours in my workshop. I can't be in the house all the time, so you kids have to show Mom and me that you can get along—"

"Without Dad around to referee every minute," Mom finished his sentence.

"Fine," said Alex, worrying Comedy and Tragedy back and forth on the chain around her neck. "But I know Stevie's just doing this to bug me. Her heart's not really in it, and this is really important to me."

"How do you know what's in my heart? Mom, I'm not just doing this to bug her, honest! For years, this whole family has been down on me because I'm not into acting like everybody else, then when finally I am ..." I couldn't finish. My voice started to wobble.

"OK, OK," said Mom, holding up both hands. "Truce!"

Dad got up from the couch. "Girls, I think you should shake on it." Leave it to Dad to get corny on us.

"I think I smell my cupcakes burning!" I said.

"Then it's settled." He watched me until I took Alex's hand. "Now, go forth and practice for those auditions. And may the best man win," Dad said for us.

"May the best *actress* win," said Alex, a little too sweetly.

A Sisters Club Emergency

"Emergency meeting of the Sisters Club," Joey said, all out of breath, as soon as I'd pulled my cupcakes out of the oven. "Upstairs. Now."

"Did Alex say?" I asked.

"No. I said."

Joey had never called a meeting of the Sisters Club. She always just bugged Alex and me to have one. But something in her eyes made me follow her.

We all piled into Alex's room (with permission). Alex and I plopped onto her bed. Joey sat cross-legged on the fuzzy flower rug.

"Can I hold Sock Monkey?" Joey asked Alex. To my surprise, Alex handed over our mascot without arguing. Not one snotty word.

"OK, first, this meeting is officially called to order." Joey held out her finger for the triple-pinkie handshake. "Sisters, Blisters, and Tongue Twisters," said Joey.

"You know what? I've been thinking," said Alex. "We should change our motto. *Blisters* is lame."

"*Blood blisters* is kinda cool," I suggested.

"And *tongue twisters* is kinda babyish," Alex finished her thought.

"No, it isn't," Joey protested. "Besides, nothing else rhymes with *sisters*."

"Misters," said Alex.

"Kisters," I said.

"Risters."

"Listers."

"Those aren't even words, most of them," Joey pointed out.

"OK, then how about ... Lister*ine*," I said helpfully.

"Then we might as well just be the Bad Breath Club," said Joey.

All of a sudden, out of the blue, Alex turned to me, as if she'd been bursting to say something. "Why do you have to go for the play, anyway? Can't you just be happy doing the cake-off?"

So much for the truce. I was sick of her attitude. "Drop dead, Alex."

Joey jumped up, her face ghost-white. "Don't say that! Stevie! Take it back!"

"OK, OK. Calm down, freak show. I take it back."

"You two have to stop fighting," Joey pleaded, looking from Alex to me.

"She started it," I said.

"Never mind," said Alex. "Joey, is this why you called the meeting?"

"OK, I called us here because you guys have to stop acting so mean and awful to each other and make up. See this pin? You guys are going to prick your fingers and mix blood with each other and promise you'll never, ever fight again. Ever."

"Joey, I'm not going to bleed for her, so you can just forget it," said Alex.

"Don't worry. I'm not about to lose blood either," I said.

"You have to promise," Joey pleaded. "If you don't, Stevie, I'll tell Alex what kind of cupcakes you've been making. And, Alex, I'll tell Stevie all the stuff I heard you tell Sock Monkey."

"How do you know what I told Sock Monkey?" Alex asked accusingly.

"Maybe I hid under the bed and heard you when you were talking to Sock Monkey. Or maybe ... I heard it through the *heating vent*. Go ahead—ask him."

"Sock Monkey, is this true?" Alex asked. Sock Monkey nodded yes (with a little help from Joey).

"C'mon, Joey, what's this all about?" I asked.

"Nothing. You're my sisters. And you're always fighting. And think about it—one of you could die, and I don't think you should waste any more time being mad at each other. When you could die, I mean. Sisters can die, you know."

I looked over at Alex. She raised her eyebrows back at me.

"Sisters fight sometimes, Joey. It's normal."

I pointed a finger at Joey, squinting my eyes with suspicion. "Joey, did you by any chance read Chapter 40?"

"Yes."

"Without me, I mean?"

"Yes."

"You read Mom's book?"

84

"Yes."

"Joey! I told you not to! It was for your own good. Why do you think I hid the book inside a cereal box in the kitchen cupboard?" I stopped, still pointing my finger at her. "Hey, how'd you find it, anyway?"

Alex had been moving her head back and forth between us. "Wait. You mean she knows?"

I nodded.

"About Beth?"

I nodded again.

Joey stood up. Her eight-and-three-quarter-inch ponytail whipped around from side to side, and she was madly waving her hands at us. "I know, OK? Beth dies. You lied to me, Stevie. You said you'd read me Chapter 40, and it wasn't even the real true story."

"It's just a book, Joey," Alex said. "A story. It's not real."

"It is to me."

"I'm sorry, Duck. I was wrong," I told my little sister. "I just knew how sad it would make you if Beth died, and I didn't want you to be sad."

"Blast and wretch. Now I'm sad, but I'm kinda mad, too."

"Joey, think of it as Shakespeare," said Alex. "Like *Romeo and Juliet.* It's a tragedy."

"Yeah, Duck, at least Beth didn't fling herself on top of a dagger or get her head chopped off."

"She just closed her eyes and went to sleep, right?" said Alex.

"Yep. See, aren't you glad? Because getting her head chopped off would be bad. Then you'd have to feel sad and mad and bad."

"I do anyway."

"Want to go downstairs and put the book back in the cereal box?" I asked Joey, thinking it might make her feel better. "Wait. You can't. We still have seven chapters left to read. Seven *happy* chapters."

"Yeah, Duck, only one more person dies."

"What? Who? Not Laurie. Please don't say Laurie. Or Jo. Wait, don't tell me!"

"Al-ex!" I said. Sometimes my big sister could be so dense.

"Sorry," said Alex. "But Stevie's right. Lots of good stuff happens. People get married and have babies and pick apples and all kinds of stuff."

"Hey, stop telling me. *'Twinkle, twinkle, little star,'*"

Joey sang, covering her ears until Alex stopped.

"And there are still three sisters left. Like us. You, me, and Alex."

"I still think you should prick your fingers and exchange blood and promise you'll never fight again."

"We can't promise, Duck. Even the sisters in *Little Women* fight."

"Yeah, Jo and Amy are always fighting and mad at each other. Remember when Amy burns Jo's book she's writing? But they always make up again."

Joey made a sour face. "Sisters, Kisters, and Listerine," she said in her blast-and-wretch voice.

Top Ten Songs NOT to Sing at an Audition, According to Stevie

by Joey Reel Top 10 Songs That Will Make a Director Throw Up and Never-Ever Pick You Because He's Heard These Songs So Many Times ~S

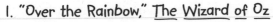

1. "Over the Rainbow," <u>The Wizard of Oz</u>
2. "Maria," <u>The Sound of Music</u>
3. "Tomorrow," <u>Annie</u>
4. "Memory," <u>Cats</u>
5. "I'm Gonna Wash That Man Right Outta My Hair," <u>South Pacific</u>
6. "In My Own Little Corner," <u>Cinderella</u>
7. "Popular," <u>Wicked</u>
8. "Good Morning Baltimore," <u>Hairspray</u>
9. "Bye Bye Birdie," <u>Bye Bye Birdie</u>
10. "Part of Your World," <u>The Little Mermaid</u>

BYE BYE ALEX
Starring Alex

Me: *(Knock, knock.)* Hey, guys, are you doing
anything?

Stevie: Yes. Yes, we are. But it's none of
your beeswax.

Me: Whatever. I just need to borrow Joey.

Joey: What for?

Stevie: You can't. She's too sad. About
Beth—you know. *(Fakes tears streaming
down face, but Joey is smiling.)*

Me: That was two days ago! *(Digging toe
into carpet.)* Joey said she'd help me pick
a song for my audition.

Joey: I'm right here!

Stevie: Well, for your information, she's
helping *me* right now.

Joey: I am. I'm helping her. But I could
help you ... *to-mor-row. (Grins, looking
over at Stevie, and points to notebook.)*

Me: What? I don't get it. What's going on?

Stevie: Hey, don't look at me. I'm just

minding my own business over here *in my own little corner*. *(Stevie and Joey spray spit, laughing.)*

Me: Look, can I talk to Joey—alone—for just a sec?

Stevie: It's OK. You can say stuff in front of me. It's not like I'm going to steal your song or anything.

Me: Well, see, I know both Maria Martinez and Jayden Pffeffer will be going for the same part, and they both take Voice and they're in the chorus and Maria will sing "Over the Rainbow" just because she always does, but Jayden—

Stevie: How do you solve a problem like *Maria*? And Jayden, too. She's really *popular*.

Joey: *(Leans back on bed and howls.)*

Me: *(Impatient.)* Thanks a lot, you guys. This is so not helping.

Joey: But we *are* helping you. Honest.

Me: Yeah, right. And how is acting like preschoolers helping me?

Stevie: *(Walks over to Joey and grabs list, ripping off the top part.)* Here. We were making a list of songs. Go ahead. Take it.

Joey: But that's not even—

Stevie: *(Covering Joey's mouth.)* Never mind, Duck. Just let her have it. She says we're not helping. So now we're helping.

Me: *(Standing in doorway, looking bewildered.)* Thanks, I guess.

Joey: *(Takes away Stevie's hand.)* But that's not fair!

Alex: What's not fair?

Stevie: *(Striking Shakespeare pose.)* All's fair in love and sisters.

Me: You guys are weird, you know that?

Stevie: Go ahead. Take it. Go. *(Makes shooing-dog motion with hands.)* OK. Bye-bye, then.

Joey: *(Calling after Alex.)* Bye-bye, Birdie!

Me: *(Leaves room, taking list. Sisters behind me mumbling and grumbling—Joey saying "not fair" and Stevie telling Joey to get over it.)*

To Tell or Not to Tell

A half hour later, I was humming songs inside my head when I heard Alex's door open. I sprang up and grabbed Joey's sleeve as she waltzed down the hall, pulling her into our room and shutting the door.

"Hey, Joey. C'mere. You have to tell me. What song is Alex going to sing for the audition?"

Joey scowled at me like I had *Fink Face* tattooed across my forehead. "I can't tell you! It's a secret."

"Please? Pretty please with the World's-Best-Sister cupcakes on top? You know you're going to tell me eventually. So why not save some time and tell me now?"

"Who says I'm going to tell you?"

"You will. Because I will sit on you and tickle you to death until you give it up."

"Go ahead—I'll never tell!"

I wrestled Joey to the floor, sat on her, and pinned her arms back. "You asked for it." I let go of her arms and tickled her as hard as I could.

"OK! OK! Stop! You win!" Joey squealed. "Uncle! I call Uncle!"

"So you'll tell me?"

"On one condition. You have to tell me *your* song. That way, I still get to know a secret that nobody else knows."

"OK, you first." I leaned down so Joey could whisper in my ear. "Alex is singing 'I'm Gonna Wash That Man Right Outta My Hair.'"

"No way! That song is on the list! The list of songs that make directors throw up! I am SO going to get this part!" I said gleefully, rubbing my hands together and grinning like Cinderella's evil stepsister.

"Now you tell me," Joey said.

"OK, I'll give you a hint. But you have to swear on your life that you won't breathe a word, or I'll cut off your entire eight-and-three-quarter-inch ponytail when you're sleeping."

"Deal."

I looked around to make sure there wasn't a spy (a.k.a. Sherlock/Alex) listening, then leaned over again and whispered "The Glory of Love" in Joey's ear.

"I know a secret! I know a secret!" Joey sang.

"Shh!" I said, covering her mouth and looking around furtively. "Do you really want to get tickled to death again?"

20 Questions
by Joey Reel

Alex is trying to guess Stevie's song:

1. Is it from a musical?
   No.
2. Is it a hymn, like "Amazing Grace"?
   No.
3. Is it "Amazing Grace"?
   No!
4. Is it a Beatles song?
   No.

Amazing Joey

5. Is it funny?
   No.
6. Is it slow or fast?
   It has to be a yes-or-no question!
7. Do I even know the song?
   YES!
8. Is it a Dylan song?
   No.

9. Is it rap? Hip-hop? Jazz? Blues?
   That's four questions! But no.

13. Does it rhyme?

Yes.

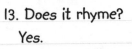

← thyme

14. Is it "Yesterday"?

I said (!) it's not a Beatles song!

15. Is it a song we learned when we were kids?

Yes!

16. Is it "Twinkle, Twinkle, Little Star"?

No. But you're getting warm.

17. "Row, Row, Row Your Boat"?

Nope.

18. "Hush, Little Baby"?

Nope.

19. So it rhymes, and we knew the song
when we were kids?

Yes. That counts as a question. One more.

20. OK, OK... Did Mom sing it to us?

YES!

"I got it! 'Sammy Was a Sailor'! Ooh, I'm good.
I'm so good!"

← Joey was
a sailor

Scream and *Scream 2:* Double Feature

"La-la-la-la-la-la-la!Lo-lo-lo-lo-lo-lo-lo.Lee-lee-lee-lee-lee-lee-lee." I paced back and forth, wearing out the roses in the carpet as I warmed up my voice to practice singing for the audition. The Big Moment was only a week away.

"Me-may-mah-mo-moo—" When I paused to take a breath, I couldn't help hearing music blaring, coming from Alex's room. And singing.

I listened in the doorway. Alex was playing musicals on the karaoke machine and singing along with them. Not softly, I might add.

"Will you read some more *Little Women* with me?" Joey asked, bounding up the stairs. Now that she had recovered from the shock of Beth's death, she was bugging me to read again.

"Not now, Joey. I'm practicing." Back in my room, I sang my scales a little louder. *"Ah-ah-ah-ah-ah-ah-ah."*

Just as I was getting into it, I couldn't help but hear Alex trying to drown me out by singing the "Maria" song from *The Sound of Music*. I tried to fight back by howling "The Star-Spangled Banner," but it was no use.

Breathe in. Don't clench your jaw. Loosen your neck. I tried to relax. I shook my arms. I wiggled my head back and forth. I closed my eyes and tried to concentrate on breathing. But Alex had cranked up the karaoke machine, singing along to every musical under the sun, just to annoy me and get my attention, I'm sure. One minute she was washing some man right out of her hair, and the next she was bragging about Oklahoma at the top of her lungs.

"Plpp, plpp, plpp, plpp, plpp, plpp, plpp." I practiced my lip rolls, up and down the scale, like a trumpet player. Next thing I knew, she was singing that she was shy, had always been shy, and had to confess that she was shy. More like screaming. She sure wasn't *shy* about letting me know she was practicing for the audition, too.

For an old tumbledown house, these walls were paper-thin. I could hear Joey in Alex's room now. They were both singing songs from musicals, screaming at the top of their lungs. I guess the Victorians who built this place did not have sisters.

I tried the under-the-covers trick. The pillow-over-the-head trick. My iPod headphones. My swimming earplugs. Joey's Oregon State Beavers earmuffs. But nothing, not even humming with fingers pressed to both ears, could drown out the Super-Screechy Soprano Sisters who'd gone *South Pacific* on the other side of the wall.

I took my fingers out of my ears to listen. "Sisters, sisters ..."

That did it! Alex wasn't even practicing anymore. Now she was getting Joey to sing the sisters song from *White Christmas* just to bug me on purpose. I paced in circles around the rug in our room, my face growing hot. So what if she's my sister? I was determined to beat her fair and square.

Me: *(Knocking on wall.)* I can hear you guys!
Them: *"Caring, sharing, blah blah blah blah*

blah blah blah blah ..."

Me: *(Louder.)* I CAN HEAR YOU!

Putting my fingers in my ears didn't help. I could still hear them singing together, acting as one ... so I gave up. Who could drown out two sisters singing the sisters song without the third sister?

"Nonny-nonny, noony-noony, no-no-no, nee-nee-nee, nay-nay-nay," Joey sang, twirling back into our room.

"Not you, too." I scowled at Joey. "Why are you helping Alex?"

"Who says I'm helping Alex? We were just goofing around."

Alex cranked up the music again. "Isn't she done yet?" I asked. "I can't hear my own voice. Joey, ask Alex to turn the music down."

"Loud music is a teenage thing. I read about it in one of Alex's magazines."

"C'mon, Joey. Go and ask."

"Why me? You ask her."

"You know she won't do it if I ask her."

"Sheesh. Do I have to do everything around here?"

"As if."

Joey headed back to Alex's room. *Mumble, mumble.* I heard voices, but I couldn't tell what they were saying. Geez! Just when you *want* to hear through these walls ...

Joey came back. "Alex said no."

"Did you ask right?"

"How should I know?"

"Joey, ask her again and this time say please, and if she still says no, tell her she's being a selfish brat and I can't hear myself think, let alone sing."

Joey left. More mumbling. She came back and plopped onto her bed.

"Well, what did she say?" I asked.

"You really want to know? She said, 'Tell Stevie calling someone a selfish brat is not the best way to get them to do you a favor.'"

"OK, this time remind Alex that I have every right to practice and sing just as much as she does."

Joey left and came back again. "Can't you just go downstairs and practice?"

"Did Alex say that?"

"Yes. But I told her to."

"Joey! Tell Alex her music is as loud as the fire alarm next door. Why should I get kicked out of my own room just because she's a Number-One Fink Face?"

"This is really confusing, you know. Just go and talk to her yourself. Tell her you'll give her ten dollars to turn down the music or something."

"You know I don't have ten extra dollars. I'm still trying to get a hundred dollars so I can be in the cake-off."

"Send an e-mail. Paper airplane. Smoke signal. I don't know. But I do know I'm getting tired of going back and forth and back and forth. What am I, a Human Ping-Pong Ball?"

"I wish you'd just go and ask her one more time," I whined.

"You know what I wish?" Joey said. "I wish I had three wishes on Dad's genie lamp and that *all three* wishes would be for everybody to stop fighting or singing or whatever and pay some attention to me for a change."

"'My patience, how blue we are!'" I said, getting Joey's attention by saying *Little Women* stuff.

"Please can we finish *Little Women*? Did you know

Jo gets Plumfield? And she opens a school for boys?"

"Wait. How did you know? Hey, you've been reading ahead."

"So? I still want us to finish it together."

"Tell you what. Listen to me sing my song for the audition, and then we'll read the last two chapters straight through."

"Swear?"

"I swear."

"Swear on *Little Women*." Joey held out the book in front of me. "Put your hand on the book and repeat after me."

"Joey!"

"Just do it."

"OK, OK." I placed one hand on *Little Women* and raised my other hand.

"I, Stevie Reel ..." Joey started.

"I, Stevie Reel ..."

"Do solemnly swear ..."

"Do solemnly swear ..."

"That I will finish reading *Little Women* ..."

"That I will finish reading *Little Women* ..."

"Help Joey with her school project ..."

"Hey, did I say I'd help with homework?"

"Cheerfully measure Joey's ponytail whenever she asks …"

"Cheerfully measure Joey's ponytail even though it's been eight-and-three-quarters inches long forever …"

"Hey! That's not what I said."

"Hey! That's not what I said," I repeated after Joey.

"And stop acting like a turd muffin."

"And stop acting like a turd muffin, whatever that is. Hey, wait, that's like four things! All I said was that I'd read—"

"Too late. You swore. On *Little Women*."

Call Me Jo!
by Jo-ey Reel

7 = chapters in <u>Little</u> <u>Women</u> after Beth dies (so sad)

0 = chapters left to read in <u>Little</u> <u>Women</u> (even sadder)

Too many to count = number of times I cried in <u>Little</u> <u>Women</u>

57 = number of times I've asked Stevie to call me Jo

1 = number of times Stevie actually called me Jo

1 = number of times Jo should have married Laurie!

5 = number of books by Louisa May Alcott I'm going to hurry up and read, starting with <u>Little</u> <u>Men</u>

Are You a Meg,

1

If you could meet one of these famous women, who would it be?

a. Michelle Obama
b. Amelia Earhart
c. Princess Diana
d. Georgia O'Keeffe

2

If you were stranded on a desert island, which book would you choose to have with you?

a. *Little House on the Prairie*
b. *Harriet the Spy*
c. *Charlotte's Web*
d. *Judy Moody*

3

How would you describe your closest friends?

a. Loyal and dependable
b. Exciting and imaginative
c. Caring and empathetic
d. Funny and creative

4

What would you consider your most embarrassing moment?

a. Waking up to find you're wearing your bathrobe at the mall
b. Accidentally walking into the boys' bathroom
c. Tripping and falling when carrying your lunch tray in front of everybody in the cafeteria
d. Telling a joke onstage and nobody laughing

Jo, Amy, or Beth?

5 **If you're snowed in at a mountain cabin, what items would you hope to have with you?**
a. A hairbrush, a toothbrush, and glitter nail polish
b. A journal, a pencil, and a candle
c. A sleeping bag, a teddy bear, and a first-aid kit
d. A cell phone, an iPod, and a pillow

6 **What's your perfect vacation?**
a. Camping at a lake under the stars
b. Skydiving
c. Staying at home and curling up with a good book
d. Visiting Monet's garden in France

- -

If you chose mostly a's, you are: MEG.
Like Meg, you are responsible and practical and have a solid head on your shoulders. You are a good listener. You are concerned with your appearance and fall in love easily.

If you chose mostly b's, you are: JO.
Like Jo, you are something of a tomboy, always getting into trouble. You are strong-willed, outspoken, know your own mind, and are quick-tempered. You are full of passion, especially for acting and writing.

If you chose mostly c's, you are: BETH.
Like Beth, you are quiet, kind, and gentle, with never a harsh word for anybody. You are generous to a fault, always thinking of others. You love animals and playing the piano.

If you chose mostly d's, you are: AMY.
Like Amy, you are funny and entertaining and like to play jokes on others. You are sometimes spoiled and given to tantrums when you don't get your way. You are an artist and a world traveler.

Break a Leg

D-day. Day of the Audition.

I was in the kitchen that morning before school, gulping down a cupcake over the sink, when Dad caught me.

"Stevie, honey. First rule of acting? Eat a good breakfast."

"Can't. In a hurry. Too nervous," I said between bites.

"Just remember to breathe," Dad said for like the one-millionth time.

"Bye, Dad. Mwa." I air-kissed him, then picked up my backpack and headed out the door.

"Have a nice trip!" Dad called after me. The Reel family equivalent of *Break a leg*.

* * *

Mom drove us to school that day. After we dropped Joey off, Alex and I were especially quiet in the car. I tried to hum my song inside my head without actually moving my lips or making a sound.

I couldn't help glancing over at Alex, wondering if she was silently practicing her song in her head, too. "Your lips are moving," I reported.

"So?" She scrunched her nose at me, chipmunk-style.

"For your information, when you do that, you look like Alvin the Chipmunk."

"Girls. Don't start." Mom pulled up to the curb in front of the school.

"Mom, don't say it," I pleaded.

"Don't say what?" she asked innocently.

"You know, the speech," I said.

"May the best man win and all that," said Alex.

"And remember," I added, imitating Mom, "no matter what happens, you're sisters."

"Oh, and sisters last a lot longer than any old play," said Alex. "Sisters are forever." I chimed in on that last part, so we both said the same thing at the same time.

"Very funny," said Mom. "This may surprise you, but I did not have a speech prepared."

"Yeah, right," Alex and I said at the same time again, cracking up. It felt good to be on the same side for once. To be laughing with my sister.

As I headed down the hall to the sixth-grade lockers, Alex called after me, "Good luck, Sailor!" I couldn't help wondering if it was a dig. But I don't think so. Even though she called me *sailor,* I thought I caught a glimpse of the old Alex somewhere in there.

Forget about concentrating. The morning was over and I barely remembered it. Lunch was a blur. And my Something-Black-from-Alex's-Closet audition-shirt that I'd ripped off from Alex's closet seemed to mock me every time I opened my locker. I couldn't help feeling a twinge of guilt about Alex. It wasn't just the shirt. I was partly responsible for the fact that she'd picked a song that was going to make the drama coach go *Gag me with a spoon.*

At the end of the day, Olivia came up behind me as

I slammed my locker shut. "Are you OK?" she asked. "You look a little green."

"I think I'm going to throw up. Why didn't you talk me out of this? Tell me I'm nuts. I can't act. What was I thinking? Acting gives me hives! Do I have hives? Be honest. Are there ugly red hivey splotches all over my face? There are, aren't there?"

Olivia leaned in and inspected my face up close. "OK, Stevie. You are officially and completely splotch-free. No red marks, except for maybe a touch of strawberry sticky stuff from that Fruit Roll-Up you had at lunch." She pressed her thumb to my cheek and rubbed.

"Ouch!" I exaggerated massaging my face.

"OK, you have *got* to chill. Take a deep breath."

"I wish everybody would quit telling me to breathe when I can't breathe."

"Relax," Olivia said. "Nobody else has a voice like yours, so just be you."

Just be you. Just be you, I repeated to myself.

"Remember that song we used to sing in first grade with Miss Tamuchi? 'This Little Light of Mine.'"

"'I'm gonna let it shine,'" I sang.

"Exactly."

ONCE UPON AN AUDITION
Starring Alex (but really Stevie)

Me: *(Sitting in the audience with Scott and other Drama Club kids, waiting for my name to be called.)* Are you nervous?

Scott: Are you?

Me: *(Giggling.)* No fair. I asked you first. But, yes, I'm nervous.

Scott: Look, my hands are sweating. *(Touches hand to mine!)*

Me: Yeah, but you'll be great. You always get up there and nobody can tell. Except for when you keep wiping those sweaty hands down the sides of your pants.

Scott: I do not!

Me: *(Smiling.)* Just kidding. I wish you were trying out for the prince, though. *(So we'd finally get to kiss!)*

Scott: Prince Dauntless? No way. He's a total geek.

Me: I know, but ... *(but then we'd be*

together, in all the same scenes) you
wouldn't have to play him that way.

Scott: Yah-huh. That's his character. Even
Mr. Cannon said he's like a bumbling
idiot.

Me: *(Say you don't care. Say that's the part
you want. Say it'll be fun.)* You never
know—it might be fun to play a bumbling
idiot for a change. You know, kind of
slapstick.

Scott: No way. I'd much rather be Sir Harry.
You should try out for Lady Larken. Then
we'd be in all the same scenes.

Me: *(Heart leaps—he wants to be in all the
same scenes!)*

Scott: So we could practice together and
everything, I mean.

Me: Oh. *(So that's all he meant.)* Shh! Here
she comes.

Scott: Here who comes?

Me: My sister! I told you she was trying out.

Scott: *(Leans forward in his seat.)* Oh,
yeah. The one who cooks, and bugs you,

and is always getting in your stuff?
She was good that time in *Beauty and
the Beast*. *(Glances over at me and sees
my frowning face.)* I mean, she was OK,
I guess.

Me: *(Whispering.)* She's never done a cold
reading before. She looks scared, like
the microphone might bite her.

Scott: Everybody's nervous at first.

Me: *(Sliding down in seat.)* Mr. C said to
act like a spoiled princess. She sounds
like a squeak toy—you know, for dogs.

Scott: Ouch. *(Watches Stevie flail around
onstage.)*

Me: *(Half covering eyes.)* What was that?

Scott: She's pretending to slip on a
banana peel.

Me: Oh. I thought she was an octopus caught
in a snowstorm, with all those arms
flying everywhere.

Scott: That's harsh.

Me: It's time for her song. Wait till you
hear this. I actually feel kinda bad

for her. She's going to sing this really
stupid song about this sailor that our
mom sang to us when we were little.

Scott: Weird. I thought you said she has a
really good voice.

Me: Yeah, but this song is so lame. It's like
a tongue twister!

Scott: Think she'll get through something
like that onstage, under the spotlight,
when she's all nervous?

Me: *(Duh.)* We'll see!

Mr. Cannon: Stevie, go ahead and give your
sheet music to Mrs. Kowalick and she'll
accompany you on the piano. Tell us what
song you've chosen, where it comes from,
and why you picked it.

Stevie: *(Clearing throat.)* Hi, um. I'm going
to be singing ...

Me: *(Squinting.)* Hey, is that my ... ?
I think she has on my black shirt! What
a little—

Scott: I can't even hear her.

Me: Told you. Microphon-o-phobia!

Mr. Cannon: We can't hear you, Stevie.
Your feet should be on that line there.
Stand right on the yellow tape and speak
directly into the mike. OK, start again.

Me: *(Covering eyes.)* She doesn't even know
to stand on the tape. I can't watch. Tell
me when it's over.

Stevie: I chose this song because it means
a lot to me. It's a song I remembered that
my mom used to sing to me when I was
little.

Mrs. Kowalick: Ready? *(Nods to Stevie.)*

Stevie: *(Swallowing.)* "You've got to give
a little, take a little, and let your poor
heart break a little ..."

Scott: *(Looks at Alex curiously, one
crinkled eyebrow raised.)*

Me: Huh? *(Sitting up straight, nervously
sliding drama mask charm back and forth
on chain.)*

Stevie: "That's the story of ... that's the
glory of ... love."

Scott: *(Nudging me in the elbow and*

whispering.) Hey, she's good.

Stevie: "You've got to laugh a little, cry a little ..." *(Hush falls over room. Not a person speaks. Not a chair squeaks. Not even a hiccup.)*

Me: Wow.

Stevie: *(Holding microphone stand, closes eyes and leans back.)* "Yes, and always have the blues a little ..."

Scott: Microphon-o-phobia, huh?

Stevie: *(Slow and sweet.)* "That's the story of ... that's the glory of ... love." *(Holds note and draws it out.)*

Me: *(Getting goose bumps, swiping at tear with back of fist.)*

Scott: A stupid song about a sailor, huh?

Me: I don't know what to say. *(I'll get that Joey for not telling me!)*

Scott: Wow. She was amazing. It's like, she takes your heart, and, I don't know, squeezes it or whatever. Wow.

Me: *(Gripping Tragedy charm on necklace.)* That's my sister. Voice of an angel.

Mr. Cannon: Take five, people.

Me: *(Opening hand, looking at charm, realizing Comedy is missing! Looking all around on floor.)* 'Scuse me. Sorry. Can I get past? *(Drama Club people mumble: "That's Alex's sister? Wow. Who knew she could sing like that, huh?")* Excuse me. Sorry. Excuse me. I've got to go. *(Retracing my steps up the aisle.)*

Once Upon an
Audition, Part Two

After my audition, my heart was still thumping, and the knot in the middle of my chest didn't melt right away. I kept turning the experience over and over in my mind as I sat in the audience with Olivia, who had promised to be my One Friendly Face at the audition.

"Stop biting your nails," Livvie said. "You're making *me* nervous."

Alex was somewhere in the back of the theater with all her Drama Club friends, but it was so dark back there, I couldn't tell which propped-up pair of flip-flops on the seat backs was my sister's.

Now that I had officially tried out for a part in a play, I had become Instant Drama Critic. Livvie and I must have sat through twelve or thirteen auditions, whispering stuff and scribbling notes back and forth.

Max Somebody: Lose the hat, dude. Eye contact!
Jayden Pffeffer: Great actress. Singing voice like a seagull.
Girl singing "Jingle Bell Rock": What were you thinking?

Then I heard Mr. C call Alex's name. She came on-stage in this emerald-green knee-length dress thing she had on over jeans, her dark, glossy curls shining in the spotlight, her sea-green eyes smiling. For her cold reading, she read from the script as easily as if we were sitting at home around the breakfast table reading the cereal box.

Mr. C asked her to act like a bossy mother. Court jester. Mute king. Bumbling idiot. Alex did it all.

Mr. C asked her to act like a spoiled princess.

She doesn't even have to act for that one! I wrote, passing my notebook to Olivia.

When the cold reading was over, it was time for Alex to do her song. I explained to Olivia about the Top Ten Songs Not to Sing list. "Here it comes," I whispered. "Time for Mr. Cannon to roll his eyes and stick his finger down his throat like he's puking." I mimed Mr. Cannon throwing up, and Olivia almost lost it.

"Mr. Cannon," I heard Alex say. "I just need a quick costume change. It will only take two seconds—I promise."

"Costume change?" I said. "I never thought about a costume. Were we supposed to have a costume?"

"What's her costume?" Olivia wanted to know.

"How should I know?" I said, zeroing in on my cuticle and biting it.

"She's *your* sister."

Alex glided onstage looking like the goddess Psyche in pink butterfly pajamas and fuzzy slippers, a fuchsia feather boa draped around her neck.

I sat up straight. *Was that dripping wet hair?*

When Alex sashays onto a stage, it makes everybody sit up a little taller, lean in a little closer. She has a way about her. My dad calls it stage presence. It means smiling, looking out over your audience, and keeping going even if you feel like you're about to hurl.

Oh, and something about good posture, too.

I could never do what Alex did. I would (a) die of embarrassment in my pajamas, (b) slump like a camel, and (c) trip on that feather boa for sure!

"What happened to her hair?" Olivia asked.

But before you could say *moat swimmer,* Alex squeezed shampoo from a bottle into her hand. She exaggerated lathering it up on her head until it was all foamy and sudsy, and just as I was beginning to wonder if my sister had seriously lost it, she started singing: "'I'm gonna wash that man right outta my hair.'"

At first, she sort of half spoke, half sang, then she pantomimed actions, which had everybody laughing. She even threw in a few funny dance steps in her slippers.

Brilliant, really. Because as I watched her and I was laughing, I almost forgot about her singing, which wasn't half bad. Way better than Fluffernutter (Jayden Pfeffer). Over the years, I had seen my sister as Annie, as Dorothy, as Beauty, as Mushroom in the Rain. I'd even seen her in an honest-to-goodness, for-real shampoo commercial when she was like three.

Stage presence. Alex sure got extra helpings when they passed that around.

There were three auditions to go after Alex. Then, just like that, it was over, and Mr. Cannon was up onstage, making an official announcement.

"I realize that it's customary to wait and post a list with callbacks, but since you're all here and we have some extra time, I'd like to ask a few of you to stay behind. If I call your name, please come and see me."

I shifted in my seat, dropped my notebook, sat on my hands.

"The rest of you are free to go. The cast list will be posted outside my office on Wednesday at three p.m. Thanks for coming in, everybody. Great job, people." He went down the list on his clipboard, calling out names.

Nathan Holabird. Jayden Pffeffer. Alvin Albertson. Zoe DuFranc. And Stevie Reel.

"That's you!" squealed Olivia beside me.

I couldn't trust my own ears. "Are you sure he said Stevie Reel? Not Alex?" I asked.

"No. You. Go, girl!" said Olivia.

My heart was thumping through my stolen shirt as I scurried up to the stage. But it pounded even harder when I got to the front of the theater and saw the back of Alex rush up the aisle and disappear out the door marked EXIT.

COMEDY LOST
Starring Alex

Me: *(Standing with back against wall in hallway, willing myself to breathe, breathe, breathe.)*

Scott: Hey, Shakespeare? You OK?

Me: *(Don't freak out. Don't. Freak. Out.)* Sorry. I'm just freaking out because I've realized I've lost half of my favorite necklace. It's kind of a good-luck charm. And then when Mr. Cannon didn't call me back ...

Scott: That doesn't mean you didn't get the part. Cannon isn't even done auditioning. He doesn't even know himself yet. Nothing's decided.

Me: *(Snapping.)* Don't you get it? *(Calm down! Be nice!)* He doesn't even have to think it over. He knew right away exactly who he wanted for callbacks—Stevie, not me. Who can compete with that voice? What was I thinking, going out there in

my pajamas with dripping wet hair? I
must be nuts. There's only one word for
me. Starts with L, ends with O-S-E-R.

Scott: You were great up there today. You
nailed it. I know you were all super-
scared, but it was good. And funny.

Me: *(You're just saying that 'cause you like
me.)* You're just saying that.

Scott: No way. I mean it.

Me: You mean it? Really?

Scott: Look, I'm out here in the hall with
you, aren't I?

Me: So?

Scott: So, I'm not in there. *(Nods towards
theater.)*

Me: So ...

Scott: Duh. I didn't get a callback either.

Me: Oh, sorry! I'm such a jerk face! I
was only thinking about myself, and
I forgot—

Scott: No biggie. Don't sweat it. I really
screwed up a couple of times on the
cold read and had to start over. Maybe

I should have tried out for Dauntless, like you said.

Me: How come?

Scott: *He's* a doof; *I'm* a doof ...

Me: Not you, too. What a pair, huh? *(Squeezing out a hunk of wet hair.)*

Scott: Hey, got an umbrella? You're dripping on me!

Me: *(Doing it again, on purpose this time.)* Well, don't worry. You're going to make a great Sir Harry.

Scott: Thanks. *(Stares at floor.)*

Me: *(Glancing towards door.)* What do you think they're doing in there? I mean, what is *my sister* doing in there? Besides stealing not just my shirt but maybe the lead away from me!

Scott: OK, Princess Freakerella. You have got to get a grip. How could Mr. C not pick you?

Me: Um, because I can't sing?

Scott: Yes, you can. Stop saying that. You're fine. And besides, who else is brave

enough to get up there in pink pj's?
(Grinning, teasing.)

Me: *(Punches Scott on arm.)* Thanks a lot.

Scott: OK, how about this? For real.
(Looking mischievous.) The opening scene
is the swamp princess all dripping
wet, right? So ... Mr. C already knows you
look cute wet.

Me: *(Turning ten shades of red. Enter
Stevie. Saved by the door!)*

Stevie: *(Sees Alex in pj's.)* Hey. Sorry it
took so long—I see it's past your bedtime.

Me: Ha, ha. Very funny.

Scott: *(Grinning at Stevie's joke.)* Hey,
Steven. You sang great in there today.
Seriously.

Me: *(Frowning.)* What happened in there
anyway? After we left, I mean.

Stevie: Singing. Lots more singing. You
know, *Me-me-my-mo-moo* and all that.

Me: Well, anyway, Dad's probably here to
pick us up. But I have to go and get my
clothes and stuff. I left them backstage.

Scott: I've got to get going, too. Bye, you guys. Later, Alex.

Me: See you tomorrow. *(Goes back inside theater. Walks down aisle to stage and climbs stairs.)*

Mr. Cannon: Good job today, Alex.

Me: *(Shielding eyes to look out into audience.)* Oh! Mr. Cannon. I didn't see you there. I thought everybody was gone.

Mr. Cannon: Just gathering up my things. Making a few final notes so I won't forget.

Me: I forgot my stuff. I'll just grab it—can't exactly go home in my pj's, you know. *(Laughs nervously and disappears behind stage.)* Got it! *(Comes down off stage.)* You didn't by any chance find a silver charm, like one of the drama masks? Or did anybody turn one in? It's kind of important.

Mr. Cannon: Nope, sorry, but I'll keep an eye out.

Me: Thanks.

Mr. Cannon: Your sister, Stevie? I remember when she stepped in for you, in *Beauty*. That's some voice, huh?

Me: *(Dropping stuff and picking it up.)* Yeah. Who knew?

Mr. Cannon: I don't know if you had anything to do with it, but I'm certainly glad she decided to try out. We can always use a good soprano.

Me: *(Twisting and untwisting pajama top.)* Well, we weren't sure she would. She's pretty busy.

Mr. Cannon: Oh?

Me: *(Go ahead, tell him.)* Yeah. She cooks. *(Just say it!)* I mean, she's been baking a lot, cupcakes and everything, because, um ... *(Spit it out!)* She's entering the Cascade County Bake-Off, I mean Cake-Off. It's coming up in a couple of months, and it's like a really big deal. *(Traitor!)* What I mean is, it takes a lot of work and time and practice and everything.

Mr. Cannon: I see.

Me: *(No turning back now.)* So, like I said, we weren't sure she'd really try out, because of all the time, I mean *(Stop saying "I mean" ...)*, because she has this other commitment, I mean.

Mr. Cannon: Well ... good to know. Thanks, Alex.

Me: *(Flees up aisle for the second time that day, bolting for exit.)*

Drama Trauma

At dinner that night (which I did not have to cook, thank you very much), I had not even tasted one bite of Dad's famous peanut-butter spaghetti because I was so excited, chattering on about the audition to my family.

"Then Mr. Cannon asked for callbacks, and I couldn't believe my ears when he called my name. He had us sing twenty-four bars of 'Opening for a Princess,' then something from 'Shy' and one I didn't know. Then he asked me to sing parts of 'Happily Ever After' by myself." I stopped chattering when I saw that Alex had closed her eyes and was breathing hard. But Joey said it for me.

"That's Winnie's song!" said Joey. *The lead.*

Alex's fork clattered to her plate. Eating stopped. Chewing stopped. Dad paused his napkin in mid-wipe. It was like church on Thursday, the room got so quiet. Everybody stared at Alex.

"What? So I dropped my fork." She picked it up, stabbed her spaghetti, twirled them in a mini-tornado, then stopped halfway to her mouth. "Can we please just talk about something else?" she pleaded.

I fell silent, biting back my enthusiasm. I looked hopefully from Mom to Dad and back. Nobody seemed to know what to say. I guess it was up to me, Stevie the Peacemaker, to say something, anything, that might break the tension.

"Alex was great today. You should have seen her. I don't know how you can get up there, in your pajamas, and not feel self-conscious. And the song, with the shampoo thing—"

"Yeah, right. My voice was literally shaking."

"I couldn't tell. It sounded like you had some good vibrato."

"I said *[stab]*, can we please *[stab]* not talk about it *[stab-stab-stab]*?" She was attacking her spaghetti again.

"How're things going at the station?" Dad asked Mom, careful not to cause any more spaghetti deaths.

Mom looked relieved for the change of subject, but it wasn't good news. "Ratings are still down. We're going to finish taping the spring season, but I think it's only a matter of time till *Fondue Sue* gets the ax. I'm sure they're not going to renew for the fall."

"Why not?" Joey asked.

"There's been such an explosion of cooking shows lately, it's hard to compete."

"I like that funny guy who goes 'Bam!'" Joey flicked her napkin over her shoulder, imitating the guy.

"*Iron Chef* is my favorite, hands down," said Dad. "That Morimoto is one lean, mean cooking machine."

"What about the woman who does all the thirty-minute meals? I like her Crunchy Chicken Toes. Yum!" I added.

"See? My own family. You're all traitors," Mom teased.

"You can say that again," Alex mumbled, squinting at me.

"And the latest is," Mom continued, "the Bus-Riding Gourmet."

133

"He cooks on a bus?" Joey asked.

"If you can believe it, it's a guy out of Portland who rides around on a free bus, stopping at restaurants along the city bus line to interview chefs and cook with them."

"All you need is a bus," I joked.

"The *Fondue Sue*–mobile," said Joey.

"Mom," I said, "maybe if you thought up a way-good original idea, the station wouldn't be able to say no, and they'd have to let you do some more shows."

"You need a slogan," said Dad. "You know, a trademark, like Joey's guy. 'Bam!' or 'It's a good thing.' Something catchy."

"Aren't those just gimmicks?" Mom asked.

"I've got it!" I said, suspending a forkful of spaghetti in midair. "You could do weird family meals like Dad's peanut-butter spaghetti."

"Gross," said Alex. Everybody stared at her again. "No, I mean, yours aren't gross or anything, Dad, but they might be to other people outside this family, I mean."

"I'm afraid Alex may be right," said Dad.

"How about cupcakes?" said Joey. "Stevie could

134

hook you up with like a million recipes."

"Thanks, honey, but the country's so health-conscious these days. I'm afraid they'd have to make them with spinach, or carrots, or beetroot."

"Spinach cupcakes! Bluck!" said Joey.

"When Olivia went to New York, they ate at this really fancy restaurant where the grilled cheese cost like fifty dollars. Maybe you could do something with fancy grilled cheese?"

"Great idea, but I'm afraid the Bus-Riding Gourmet had already beaten me to the grilled cheese idea. That's his first show."

"Maybe if you came up with a new name for your show," I suggested. "Admit it, Mom, *Fondue Sue* is lame."

"I've got it!" Joey squeaked. "The Ultimate Extreme Food Makeover Show!"

We brainstormed more ideas for Mom, and soon the conversation turned to Dad and the magic flying carpet he was building for *Aladdin*. Joey nearly stood up on her chair, offering ideas of how he could get the magic carpet to fly without anybody seeing wires or anything.

"I think I'm going to take a field trip over to the Cascades Playhouse. They're doing *Scheherazade,* and I figure there's got to be a flying carpet in the story of *The Thousand and One Nights.* Maybe one of you kids would like to come along."

"Me!" Joey piped up before anyone else had a chance.

I half expected Alex to chime in, making her case for being the Actor and how she should get to go. But she didn't say anything. Not a word.

Which said an awful lot.

Princess or Porcupine
by Joey Reel

Alex and Stevie both tried out for the lead in the play today. Who will get to be Princess Winnifred? Time to do a super-duper, once-and-for-all, real Reel princess test on each sister. <u>The Princess and the Pea</u> kind, just like in <u>Once Upon a Mattress</u>.

Rules for Princess Test:
1. Put tons of stuff under each sister's mattress when they aren't looking.
2. See who can sleep and who can't.
3. A real princess can feel a pea under her mattress and can't sleep a wink.
4. Whoever can't sleep is the princess and will get the part.
5. The other sister is a ... porcupine!

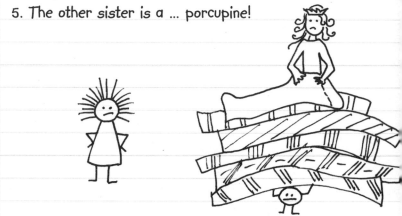

Stuff to put under Alex's and Stevie's mattresses:

- Marbles
- Rocks
- Stuffed animal chipmunk or hedgehog
- Dictionary or encyclopedia!
- Sock balls
- Pinecones

Stuff NOT to put under mattresses:

- A pea!

Stuff found under Alex's mattress:

- Magazines! More quizzes!

Stuff found under Stevie's mattress:

- Dust bunnies
- Sock lint
- Crumbs
- Old maids (popcorn kernels, not cards)
- No diary

Pinecones and Pincushions

After dinner and homework, I stretched out on my bed, arms behind my head, humming happily to myself, rehearsing songs from the play in my mind, something I'd been doing a lot ever since I'd decided to try out. I kept going over the audition in my head, smiling and trying not to bite my nails.

Joey looked over at me. "You hum as much as Mr. Brooke when he started to fall in love with Meg."

"A person can hum and not be in love, Joey." Suddenly, I felt something. A lump. A bump. A hump, under my back.

I reached my hand down under the mattress and felt around. A rock. A Lego piece. A pinecone? I yanked on one of Joey's stuffed animals, pulling it out by the ear.

"Hey, Joey? Why is there a mountain of stuff under my bed?"

"Huh? What mountain? Where? I didn't put a mountain under your mattress. It wasn't me. Honest."

"Jo-ey?"

"OK. I give up. I might have put a couple of things under there."

"A couple of things?" I hopped off my bed and lifted up the mattress, pointing. Marbles and magazines. Rocks and sock balls and stuffed animals. "You call this a couple of things? There's like a whole museum under there."

Joey giggled. "You crumb bum—you weren't supposed to find any of that stuff before you went to sleep tonight."

"No kidding." I pulled out two Scottie-dog magnets, a bag of squished potato chips, and a big, fat dictionary.

"Don't take it out. Leave it."

"I'm not sleeping on a junk heap. What's going on?"

"OK, aren't you dying to know who's going to get the part of princess? You or Alex?"

"Yes. But what's all this junk got to do with it?"

I asked, tossing a pinecone, two sock balls, and a stuffed animal at Joey.

"It's a test. A princess test. To see who's the princess. The one who can't get a good night's sleep is the real princess. That's who's going to get the part."

"Joey, you're crazy, you know that?" I stretched back out on my bed. This time it was smooth, not bumpy. No more pinecones.

"If it makes you feel any better, I did it to Alex, too."

"Only a little better," I said, taking aim at Joey with the stuffed chipmunk.

THE WEIRD SISTERS
Starring Alex (But not as a Weird Sister)

Me: *(Yawn. Stretch. Wakes to smell of pancakes on Saturday morning and comes downstairs.)* Mmm! Pancakes!

Stevie: Oh, so you're speaking to me for a change. Or do you just love me for my pancakes?

Me: Pancakes.

Joey: How did you sleep, Alex?

Me: Huh? Oh, great. Wonderful. Terrific. Like a princess! *(Stevie coughs, and Joey spits a blueberry across the room.)*

Me: What? What's wrong with that?

Stevie: *(Can hardly keep from laughing.)* Nothing.

Joey: *(Laughing.)* Nothing.

Me: *(Taking a pancake and drizzling it with syrup.)* Well, I don't see what's so hilarious about getting a decent night's sleep.

Joey: It's just that ... we thought you might ... *(Gets mad look from Stevie.)* Never mind! *(Cracks up some more.)* It's not like you had rocks under your mattress. Or marbles or pinecones or anything that would make it lumpy so
you couldn't sleep.

Stevie: Joey!

Me: No peas under my mattress. *(Joey sprays the counter with spit from laughing again.)* But, Stevie, you look like you had some under yours.

Stevie: Not me. I took them all out.

Joey: *(Mouths "Shut up!" to Stevie and runs upstairs.)*

Stevie: Doesn't matter. I still couldn't sleep at all last night. I kept tossing and turning and waking up with dreams. I can't quit thinking about the play.

Joey: *(Runs back into room, making funny faces at Stevie. Holds out hand and makes tiny circle with finger and thumb.)*

Me: You guys sure are the Weird Sisters

this morning. But who am I to guess at the strange minds of my little sisters?

Joey: The Weird Sisters. That's a good one.

Stevie: No, it's not, Joey. The Weird Sisters are the ugly hag witches from *Macbeth*.

Joey: Look out. She's going all Shakespeare on us again.

Me: *(Grinning, pleased with myself.)* "We are such stuff as dreams are made on, and our little life is rounded with a sleep."

Stevie: You're sure in a good mood this morning.

Me: And why shouldn't I be? Look out thy window, little sisters, and behold a world so lovely it bringeth a tear to mine eye.

Stevie: It bringeth a gag to mine throat when you start making up Shakespeare.

Joey: What's so great about today? Besides Stevie's pancakes, I mean. How come you're not all stressed about who's getting the part?

Me: *(I glance at Stevie. Stevie steals a look at me, then pretends to be concerned*

with pancake batter.) I just have a good
feeling, that's all. (Trying to sound
casual.) Plus, today's my first voice
lesson.

Stevie: (Drops mixing spoon, which
splatters to floor in a goosh of pancake
batter.) What? (Pronounces the "t" like
she's spitting.)

Me: You don't have to spit. I just wanted to
work on my singing technique.

Stevie: Technique? How come you need a
technique? Can't you just open your mouth
and sing like the rest of the people on
the planet?

Me: I need to be ready for when I get the
part. (Throws back head in glam pose,
shaking hair.)

Joey: Not again, you guys. (Holds hands
over ears.) Don't forget about Beth.
Chapter forty. Little Women. You
promised.

Me: We didn't promise.

Stevie: Give me back my pancake.

145

Me: *(Stops mid-bite.)* Are you crazy? I've already eaten half of it. What is *wrong* with you? *(Stevie takes half pancake, and Alex grabs it back.)*

Dad: *(Enters room.)* Girls! What's going on here?

Joey: Tug-of-war. Over a half-eaten pancake.

Dad: Alex. Stevie. That's enough. You know Mom and I don't like you wasting good food.

Stevie: Dad, you told her she could take voice lessons? But I have to beg, borrow, and steal just to enter the cake-off?

Joey: You *stole*?

Dad: *(Hands out as if to say "Slow down.")* It's not voice *lessons.* It's one lesson. And the first one's free. Alex found a flyer at school for the Voicemeister and—

Stevie: And she gets voice lessons before she even gets the part? Why does everybody just assume Alex is going to get the part? I mean, what about—I thought *I* was the singer in this family.

Me: Maybe you should take some acting lessons, little sister.

Stevie: Yeah, and maybe you should take some *sister* lessons.

Dad: Girls. I said, that's enough. You know we talked about this. *(Looking at kitchen clock.)* Alex, we leave in ten minutes, and you're still in your pajamas.

Me: Yikes! *(Grabs rest of fought-over pancake, flees upstairs.)*

Will the Real Princess Please Stand Up?

As soon as Dad and Alex had gone off to Voice Lesson Land, I took down a clean bowl and started on a new batch of cupcakes before Mom could stop me from making more mess.

I was tossing and stirring, measuring and mixing, when Joey came back into the kitchen and peered at the dark batter in the bowl. "Those are way-really weird-looking pancakes."

"They're not pancakes anymore. They're cupcakes."

"Oh, no. Do they have a name this time?"

"Oh, you mean like My-Sister-Is-a-Number-One-Fink-Face cupcakes? I-Want-to-Rip-Her-Hair-Out cupcakes?"

"My-Sister-is-Bald cupcakes. That would be funny."

"How about My-Sister-Is-Going-to-Take-Voice-Less-ons-and-Learn-How-to-Sing-Better-Than-Me-and-Ruin-My-Life cupcakes?"

"Isn't that kinda long?" Joey asked.

I kept stirring.

"Besides, it's just one teeny lesson," said Joey.

"Oh, yeah? Think about it. Dad will meet this Voice-meister guy. He's probably some struggling actor, and Dad will want to help him out. Next thing you know, Dad'll figure out some way to pay for Alex to take voice lessons and Voice Man will come over and help her night and day and she'll be the star of the play and suddenly I won't be the singer in the family anymore."

"Yeah, then I bet Alex will fall in love with the Voice Man, the same as Meg falling in love with Laurie's tutor in *Little Women,* and they'll have a wedding and get married and everything."

"Great. At least Alex will be too busy sewing and learning to make jam and doing wife stuff to be in the play."

"Ooh, ooh—and Alex will give her glove to the Voice Man, the way Meg gave hers to Mr. Brooke."

149

"I hate to break it to you, but Alex doesn't even own gloves."

"Mittens, then," said Joey.

"Forget it. It's no use. I might as well just stop thinking about singing in the play and concentrate on cupcakes," I said, furiously knocking the wooden spoon against the rim of the mixing bowl.

Joey reached over and stopped my hand. "You're going to get the part."

"Huh? You don't know that, Joey."

"Yah-huh." She mopped up every last drop of syrup on her plate with the last pancake. "I'll prove it. But you have to come upstairs."

I surrendered my spoon and followed Joey up the stairs to our room. She marched over to my bed, lifted up my mattress, and pointed. Under the mattress was a lone cat's-eye marble, sky-blue with a cloud-white ribbon running through it.

"See? Don't you get it?" Joey said.

"One marble, Joey?" I asked.

"It's like the princess and the pea. Alex had tons of stuff under her mattress and she slept like a log. But you—all you had was one little, teeny-tiny-weeny marble the size of a pea, and you said yourself that you couldn't sleep at all. You know the line from the song: 'For a princess is a delicate thing.' See? You're the sensitive one."

"Joey, just because I slept on a marble doesn't make me—"

"Yah-huh. It was a test. You passed. Alex flunked. That means you're the princess. You get the part."

"And what does that make Alex? Princess Runner-Up?"

"I don't know. I was thinking a ... porcupine."

"Porcupine, huh?"

Joey watched me as a slow smile crept back onto my face. It was just a made-up test, but I couldn't help getting a shiver. A maybe-I-have-a-real-chance-at-getting-the-part shiver.

"You've just given me a great idea, Duck. Now I know what to name my new batch of cupcakes. Want to help me?"

"What are they?"

"OK, how about pumpkin cupcakes with dark icing and almond slivers for quills. My-Sister-Is-a-Porcupine cupcakes!"

Pins and Needles

Whoever thought up pins and needles should have called it a bed of nails. Waiting all day Wednesday for Mr. Cannon to post the cast list was like sitting on a bed of nails. A Prickle of Pinecones. A Murder of Marbles.

It was way worse than a pea under twenty princess mattresses, I can tell you that. I thought three o'clock might never come. But even though the day seemed to take a year and a half, the bell finally rang.

By the time I got down to the auditorium, a Gaggle of Drama Club kids was crowded around the bulletin board outside Mr. Cannon's room. The list had been posted, but I couldn't see it. I tried standing on tiptoe and peering around this tall, skinny white eighth grader with baggy pants and a big mop of curly hair.

After lots of pushing and squinting, I spotted the name at the top of the page. It might just as well have been flashing in neon lights, because once I saw it, I couldn't stop seeing it.

PRINCESS WINNIFRED: Alex Reel.

My heart thudded. A wave of nausea hit me in the middle of my chest. My arms and legs suddenly felt heavy.

I ran my finger down the list, looking for my own name.

QUEEN AGGRAVAIN: Jayden Pffeffer
PRINCE DAUNTLESS: Alvin Albertson
LADY LARKEN: Zoe DuFranc
SIR HARRY: Scott Howell

My eyes started to blur. Maria Martinez. Kirsten Dunbar. I kept scanning down the list, but I didn't see my name anywhere.

"Hey, you got Chorus: First Soprano. That's great," said a girl next to me. I could barely eke out a simple thanks.

Chorus! After all that, I hadn't even got a real part! I was just one of a whole Shrewdness of Singers.

My ears were ringing. I tried to squeeze through the clump of tall kids in front of the bulletin board.

"Alvin's perfect for Dauntless!"

"Who's Zoe?"

"Fluffernutter was born to play Queen Aggravain."

My head was spinning. Like when you're a little kid on one of those playground merry-go-rounds and it's scary to stand up. I needed something to lean on. I went over and stood against a Raft of Lockers, hoping the solid, cold steel would prop me up. I slid down the lockers, crumpling to the floor.

I'd been doing my best not to get my hopes up, but then along came Joey's princess test, which had turned my head around.

It wasn't till my head stopped spinning that I glanced up and saw Alex. Her eyes were blazing green, but when they landed on me, they seemed to pale to an almost dull leaf brown. They were no longer the green-eyed monsters of jealousy I'd come to know so well these past few weeks.

I tried to forget my own heart-sinking disappointment for a moment, willing myself to smile. But my mouth didn't seem to be working.

My sister sprang into action. She somehow wrestled her way out of the pressing crowd and slid down next to me on the cold, hard floor of the school hallway.

Alex started talking super-fast, like the people on one of Dad's old vinyls that we used to spin by hand around the turntable so they'd sound like Alvin and the Chipmunks. "You should have at least got Larken. Or Queen Aggravain. Jayden Pffeffer can't act the warts off a toad. And that Zoe girl, what was Mr. C thinking? It's like she came out of nowhere. She's only been in Drama Club for like a few weeks and nobody even knows her."

"It's OK, Alex." I found myself comforting *her*. "You don't have to say that stuff."

"It was your first audition. Don't feel bad."

Why not?

"I'm sure Mr. Cannon wanted to give you a part.

But there were just too many other kids trying out. Seventh and eighth graders, I mean. And they've been in Drama Club longer."

Somehow, Alex cheering me up was making me feel worse.

"A big part of acting is disappointment," she said. "You deal with it."

Easy for you to say, Princess Winnifred.

"I don't know what I was thinking, anyway," I said. "I'm no actor. You really were the best up there. You deserved to get the lead."

"You mean it?"

"Yeah. I guess deep down I never really thought I'd get it. I mean, it's a musical, and you know how I like singing, and I thought there wouldn't be a lot of lines to memorize. But let's face it — acting still gives me hives."

Alex couldn't help smiling. "Well, I've got a lot of work to do on my singing. No matter how much I practice, I'll never sound as good as you."

"Hey, Shakespeare," Scott Towel called, coming over to us. "Princess Winnie. Nice going."

"You too, *Sir Harry*," Alex said, her green eyes

sparkling. "We both got the parts we wanted! Isn't it great?"

Apparently I had turned invisible. "Yeah, great," I mumbled. *Am I smiling and nodding too much?* "Just-just-just great," I heard myself say. *Stop stuttering!* "Really great." *Stop saying "great."*

"You too, Steven." Scott Towel was nodding his head like that Shakespeare bobble-head doll on Dad's dashboard, making me feel nauseous again. "First soprano. Not too shabby, huh?"

"It's just chorus. I mean, I don't even know if I'll do it."

"What do you mean you don't know?" said Alex, leaping to her feet and looking down at me like I'd just said we should set the school on fire or something. "Of course you're taking it. You worked hard for this. And you have a beautiful voice. You can't just up and quit before you even start, just because you didn't get the part you wanted."

"Chorus isn't a part at all!" I said.

"Alex is right. You can't quit," said Scott Towel. "I just bumped into Mr. C outside his office, and he said he's going to break you out of the ensemble to sing a lot of solo parts that tell the story. Like that scene when I go running off to find the swamp princess. C'mon, bail me out here, Steven. Don't make me sing up there all alone." He shook his head as if to say "Not pretty."

"I guess I could. I mean, I did try out because I wanted to sing," I said.

"Cool! It'll be like that scene we did together last year in *Beauty and the Beast.*"

"At least you won't be so hairy this time," I teased.

"Nope, just *Sir* Harry."

I couldn't help it. I cracked up.

"That's great, you two. Just great," said Alex, faking enthusiasm. Suddenly it was the Green-Eyed Monster again, not my sister, who flashed her eyes at me.

SHAKESPEARE MONKEY
Starring Alex

Sock Monkey: You are a flap-mouthed
wrinkled witch. A toad-spotted vile worm.
Lower than dirt. You are like the dirt
on the worm under the dirt.

Me: Wait a minute. Since when do you get
to start conversations? You wouldn't even
be able to talk if it weren't for me, don't
forget. So who's calling who dirt?

Sock Monkey: How can you possibly be
feeling bad? You got the part. The
lead. You beat your own sister. You beat
everybody. You win. Don't you get it?

Me: Then why do I feel so lousy?

Sock Monkey: Oh, maybe-possibly-kinda
because you ratted out your own sister?
You toad-spotted rat-nosed foot licker!

Me: Ha! Who are you, Shakespeare Monkey?
You know not of what you speak.

Sock Monkey: Yes, yes, I do. I know plenty.
I can tell when you feel guilty, and you

should—after telling Mr. Cannon that
Stevie was soooo very, very busy! Too busy
to, say, handle a *lead* role?

Me: I did not say that! I said she might
have trouble making such a big
commitment. You have to practice like
every afternoon and on Saturdays for
weeks and weeks. How can she do that
AND the cake-off?

Sock Monkey: That's not up to you.

Me: Yeah, so? It's up to Mr. Cannon. I didn't
make the rules.

Sock Monkey: No, but you know what you
said. And don't try to tell me you didn't
do it on purpose. If you hadn't said
anything, Stevie might have had a chance
at getting the lead. Then where would
you be?

Me: Can't you just shut up for once?

Sock Monkey: And still you're acting
jealous? Just because Stevie jokes around
with your boyfriend?

Me: He's not my boyfriend! And besides,

now I have to be a loud-mouthed swamp
princess and learn to sing all those
silly songs and hang out with Alvin the
Chipmunk during practice every day,
while Stevie gets to rehearse songs with
Scott Towel.

Sock Monkey: Uh! I don't want to hear it!
You know what you are? You are a beef-
witted boar pig.

Me: Ha!

Sock Monkey: Say it!

Me: I'm a beef-witted boar pig.

Sock Monkey: Well, just so you know.

Me: OK, OK. So I'm a horrible person!

Sock Monkey: And sister.

Me: And sister. *(Putting Sock Monkey on
dresser and facing him towards wall so I
don't have to look at him!)*

<u>O</u>nce <u>U</u>pon <u>a</u> Mattress
Maths Facts
by Joey Reel

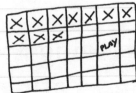

10 = number of days till <u>O</u>nce <u>U</u>pon <u>a</u> <u>Mattress</u>,
    I think

10 gazillion = number of times I have had to hear
            Alex sing "Shy"

20 = number of mattresses in <u>O</u>nce <u>U</u>pon
    <u>a</u> <u>Mattress</u>

1 = number of princess tests Alex flunked

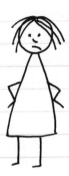

13 = number of things I put under Alex's mattress

0 = number of speaking lines Stevie
    has in <u>O</u>nce <u>U</u>pon <u>a</u> <u>Mattress</u>

Having My Cake
and Eating It, Too

The January calla lilies had rusted long ago, hanging their heads, and the February daffodils were fading, making way for March daisies. The fog had lifted, too. Green fur carpeted the hills around Acton, and the first fingertips of fir trees and redwoods reached for the almost-April Oregon sky.

Joey was all about Oregon these days. She was working on a big state project for school now. I could usually find her sprawled on the floor, surrounded by markers and colored pencils, drawing western meadowlarks (state bird) and hairy tritons (state shell). Every day now, she drank at least one glass of the Oregon state beverage (milk).

"Oregon is boring," she said one day while shading in a hazelnut.

"Ha! Oregon is so NOT boring," I told her. "We have caves and craters and Lewis and Clark, and don't forget Beverly Cleary and the Oregon Trail. You used to love pioneers. And hello! There's a volcano right outside your window."

"We don't even have a state poem," Joey said.

"So write one," I told her.

"You sound like my teacher. We have to write one as part of our project."

"See? You love writing poems," I reminded her.

"Not about boring old Oregon. You know what I wish?"

"That Louisa May Alcott had lived here?" I asked.

"You read my mind," said Joey, grinning. "Why did she have to live all the way across the map in Boston, anyway?"

My little sister still had *Little Women* on the brain.

Can I just say—it's been pretty much peaceful around here for the last several weeks. Almost too peaceful. Kind of like the calm before the storm. Joey actually counted the number of days since Alex and

I had had a fight (forty-three). Or *disagreement,* as Mom and Dad always make us call it.

I didn't see how it could stay this way—it was like one of those laws of nature, or something.

You know that feeling, how the world looks upside-down when you tip your head back really far? It was like that. Somehow my trying out for the play had tilted the axis. Not the whole earth, just our family. I had upset the balance somehow.

Once Alex got the lead (and I more-or-less got over her getting it) things went back to normal, I guess you could say. But I remember it took at least three weeks and three dozen My-Sister-Got-the-Lead cupcakes to get used to the idea.

On the first dozen, I had just wanted to smush her curly head face-first into a bowl of gooey cake batter. By the second batch, I wanted to hit her over the head with a spatula full of icing. Somewhere around Dozen Number Three of my Post-Audition Cupcake Frenzy, I tried to stop seeing my spatula as a means of revenge.

By the time I finished baking that third dozen, I was able to ice them without crushing each one to smithereens. I had finally decided I was better off not getting the lead in the play anyway. After all, by not having to be the princess in the play, I got to:

1. Still be in the cake-off
2. Not wear an ugly swamp princess dress made of dripping wet rags
3. Get out of saying stuff like "Gluggle-uggle-uggle"
4. Avoid any lovey-dovey scenes with Alvin the Chipmunk
5. Not have Alex mad at me for the rest of my natural-born life

I think I was icing Cupcake Number Thirty-Three when it hit me for the first time that I was actually happier to be in the chorus.

So, it all turned out for the best. This way, I get to do what I love: sing. And NOT do what I don't love: memorize lines and speak in front of people, which, when I really think about it, still kind of gives me hives. After all, in the chorus, I got to sing way more songs than just one puny solo. And instead of being mad at me, Alex got to be mad at Zoe DuFranc, who was playing Lady Larken and smooching Paper Towel (a.k.a. Scott).

The best thing about being in the chorus was that we didn't have to go to every single cast rehearsal or practice every day. So I sang in the chorus three times a week and the rest of the days I practiced making cupcakes because ... did I mention ... once Mr. Cannon came up with the genius idea of putting me in the chorus, I realized I had time to enter the First Annual Cascade County Cake-Off! For real! (For Reel?)

Not only did I have more time now to get ready, but I also had the rest of the money for the entry fee! After guilt-tripping Mom and Dad about letting Alex continue with voice lessons, they agreed to lend me enough money to enter. (I think they also felt bad for me that I didn't get a bigger part in the play!) So even though I'll be kissing my allowance good-bye till I'm eighteen, I was pretty pleased with myself.

I'd finally decided that my perfect cake, my masterpiece, would be an enchanted castle made entirely out of ... you've guessed it ... cupcakes! I wouldn't cheat and use a cake mold or layer cakes or sheet cakes—just

167

cupcakes. It would have at least six towers, complete with spires and windows, and a moat around it made of blue sprinkles, maybe even a working Kit Kat–and–licorice–shoelace drawbridge.

Even though I hadn't figured it all out yet, I showed Joey my rough-draft sketch and she said it kicked big gingerbread-house butt!

Oregon State Project
by Joey Reel

- **STATE BIRD:** Western meadowlark Bor—ing! ~S
- **STATE FLOWER:** Oregon grape Since when is a grape a flower
- **STATE MOTTO:** <u>Alis</u> <u>Volat</u> <u>Propiis</u>: ~S again

    "She flies with her own wings"
- **STATE NICKNAME:** ~~Groundhog state~~

    The Beaver State
- **STATE NUT:** Hazelnut STATE NUT: Alex Reel! ~S
- **STATE SHELL:** Hairy triton Sounds like a Shakespeare
- **STATE ROCK:** Thunder egg swear—Out with you,
    thou hairy triton!
- **STATE BEVERAGE:** Milk Why not chocolate milk? —me, J
- **STATE POEM:** you forgot one. ~S There isn't one. We have
- **STATE SONG:** "Oregon, My Oregon" to write one ourselv
    —J
- **FAMOUS OREGONIAN:** Cecil D. Andrus

weird! ~S
it's a geode! —J

Who? ~S Who? A.

I can't help it. I never
heard of any of them! —J

Beverly Cleary ~S

Guy who invented
The Simpsons A.

HEY, STOP WRITING
ON MY REPORT! —J

Mr. Cannon Drops a Cannonball

I went to bed and counted cupcakes. Guess what? It doesn't work like counting sheep, where cute, woolly animals leap over perfect white fences in lazy green meadows, and suddenly you yawn and drop off to Dreamland. These cupcakes might as well have had mean-guy faces, because they sure weren't lulling me to sleep.

Just the opposite.

They were keeping me awake. They were keeping me awake because I was trying to calculate whether or not I had enough cupcakes built up in the freezer for the castle I hoped to make for the cake-off on Saturday.

Saturday! Only one and a half days away.

I must have finally drifted off, because when I woke

up, it was Friday. At school that day, I doodled more cupcake castles in the margins of my notebook, trying to figure out the Grand Total number of cupcakes I would need, but I kept coming up short. Somebody (a.k.a. Joey) had obviously been stealing my Do-Not-Touch-or-I'll-Chop-Your-Hair-Off freezer cupcakes.

I even had the cake-off on my mind at play practice after school.

"Stevie, are you with us?" *Mr. Cannon.*

"I'm with you."

"You missed your cue."

I stepped out of the chorus and sang a few riffs of "Quiet," then stepped back in line.

"Great. Good," said Mr. Cannon. "Except that wasn't the verse we were on."

Oops.

"I like the energy we had on the finale today. That's exactly what I want to hear tomorrow, people. Don't forget, I want to see everybody in full costume for the final dress rehearsal. Full cast. Great work, everybody. See you then."

I turned to Samantha, the seventh-grade girl next to me. "Did he say tomorrow?"

171

"Yeah, tomorrow. You know, dress rehearsal."

"Yeah, but, I thought—"

"It's no big deal. We just have to come in costume. I guess Mr. C wants to make sure we can still sing with those big pointy hats on or something." She giggled.

"I'm dead."

"How come? What's wrong?"

"I can't come. I have something important I need to do tomorrow."

"So, just tell him. He'll understand."

"Yeah, right. Mr. Anybody-Who-Misses-a-Practice-Gets-Kicked-Out-of-the-Chorus. You know how strict he is about showing up. You're only allowed to miss like one practice."

"Have you missed any?" asked Samantha.

"No."

"So?"

"Yeah, but this is the dress rehearsal. How could this have happened?"

"I don't know. It's been on the rehearsal calendar forever. And it says full cast."

"I didn't know it meant the chorus, too. Yep, I'm officially dead."

I took an excruciatingly long time packing up my stuff. When the auditorium was empty of all other kids, I inched over to Mr. Cannon.

I cleared my throat, but my voice sounded like a mouse's anyway. "Mr. Cannon, could I maybe talk with you for a minute?"

"Sure, Stevie. Is everything OK? You seemed a bit, shall we say, distracted today. I need you to focus, and make sure you come in with your 'dragonfly's wing' line on cue."

"I know. It's not that. Look, I have to tell you something, and I know it's going to make you mad, but, see, I read the schedule and everything, and how it said full cast for dress rehearsal, but I didn't know that meant everybody. I mean, I knew it meant cast members, like actors, but I didn't know it meant the chorus, too."

"And … ?" he said, motioning with his hand for me to go on.

"And, um, well, I can't come tomorrow. See, I really like to bake and stuff, too, and I'm entering the Cascade County Cake-Off, and it's tomorrow, and I didn't know and I had to pay a hundred dollars just to be in it, and it's at the same time, so I don't see how I can—"

"Be in two places at the same time?" Mr. Cannon finished the sentence for me.

"Exactly." I let out a breath. It was a relief to have the words no longer knotted up inside me.

"Look, Stevie, I'm glad you came to me in person to let me know, but it's not the end of the world. You're my strongest soprano, and you've had these songs down for weeks."

"Really? You mean it? So it's OK if I can't be here tomorrow? I can still be in the play?"

"No worries. I was aware that this might present a problem long before now. Honestly, when I first heard that you had other major commitments, I was concerned that it might interfere with practices."

"You were?"

Mr. C nodded. "But I don't think you've missed a single practice. You've shown me you're committed to this play."

I was aware ... might present a problem ... when I first heard ... Mr. Cannon's words knocked around inside my head like blueberries in a blender.

"Wait—you mean you knew? About the cake-off? But how? Who … ?"

"Alex mentioned it to me."

"Oh. Really? When?"

"The day you auditioned, she told me it might be difficult for you to be at all the rehearsals, because you were entering the baking competition."

"You mean she told you before you decided who got the parts?"

"Yes, the day of the audition. But that's not why I put you in the ensemble, Stevie. Your voice is key to my whole chorus."

"But I … never mind. Thanks, Mr. Cannon." I picked up my backpack and slung it over my shoulder. Suddenly, it felt as heavy as two tons of concrete. I trudged up the aisle.

"Oh, and Stevie?" called Mr. C behind me. "I almost forgot. Can you give this to your sister? Its just turned up, and I know she's been looking for it." Alex's missing charm. He held it up, dangling it in the air. Comedy seemed to scoff at me.

"Oh, and one more thing," Mr. Cannon said. "Knock 'em dead at the cake-off tomorrow, kiddo."

I Know What You Did Last Winter

Quiet anger is worse than the yelling kind. With the yelling kind, you scream at your sister, "Don't talk to me again. Ever!" and after you yell, the tight fist inside you lets go, and you can breathe again.

But quiet anger is like that experiment we did in Girl Scouts in the third grade—the one where they pass out a can of soda and a nail and you think you're going to get to make some cool rocket or something. Instead, you drop a nail in a can of soda and wait to see how long it takes to rust out and fall apart. The soda slowly eats away and eats away at that nail until it dissolves and disappears.

And guess what? The nail is supposed to represent the inside of your stomach. (Needless to say, I didn't drink a soda for weeks and weeks after that experiment.)

After play practice, I felt the anger, like that nail, eating away inside me, poisoning my insides way worse than sugar and chemicals.

Alex is my sister. How could she do something so mean-awful-wicked? This wasn't like sneaking into your sister's room or peeking into your sister's diary or borrowing your sister's shirt without asking. Normal sister stuff. Petty crimes.

But this—she had actually gone and told Mr. Cannon that I would not be able to handle a big part. Even though he said that's not why he put me in the chorus, the truth was, Alex had still gone behind my back and tried to turn him against me.

So not fair!

I felt like screaming. I felt like ripping out every hair on her head. I felt like breaking down her door and yelling, *YOU ARE NOT MY SISTER*.

But I didn't.

Instead, I regarded my sister like a science experiment. The nail in the Coke. Something to watch. Observe. Maybe if I watched closely enough, it would give me a hint, a clue, an inkling, about how a person could go behind my back, betray me, break every rule of sisterhood.

Friday night.

It was time. Time to take all my cupcakes out of the freezer. *Baa, baa, black sheep, twelve bags full.* Except there weren't twelve bags full—there were only eleven, thanks to a family full of Sneaky-Pete Cupcake Snitchers.

By my calculations in the margins of my Language Arts notebook, I needed one dozen more to finish my castle. By tomorrow.

I got to work.

It felt good to bake one last and final batch of cupcakes. One perfect dozen of My-Sister-Can-Drop-Dead-and-I-Don't-Mean-Gorgeous cupcakes.

While the cupcakes were baking, I decided to work out my anger on icing. Brown icing, blue icing, white icing.

After an angry whirlwind of stirring, mixing, folding, and whipping, my tempest had subsided in a dust cloud of powdered sugar, and I was ready to begin building.

I started with the foundation, using cupcakes to form a giant rectangle for the base of the castle. Then I slathered icing across several cupcakes at a time, stacking them one on top of another on top of another until they were high enough to form walls.

The most fun was stacking cupcakes, one stack on each end, for towers and turrets, and one inside the walls for the castle keep. Upside-down ice-cream cones made perfect spires, and a licorice lace wrapped around the tower looked like a spiral staircase.

It must have been nearly midnight by the time I finished the drawbridge over the moat and crept upstairs.

My last thought as I fell asleep was not about cupcakes or castles or cake-offs.

My last thought was about Alex.

I wished I had the courage to sneak into my sister's room while she was sleeping and paint her whole face green! Then everyone would know. Her secret would be out. The whole wide world would see that my sister Alex was not a princess at all. Not even a porcupine.

My sister Alex was the Wicked Witch.

After all, wasn't it the Wicked Witch who had to have the ruby slippers, no matter what the cost?

Are You a Good Siste

Find out if you are a *super* sib,
a *so-so* sib,
or a *seriously lame*

1 **If you wore your sister's sweater and wrecked it, would you . .**
a. Buy her a new one.
b. Tell her you're sorry.
c. Hang it back in her closet and pretend you never took it.

2 **Your sister wants help with homework. You . . .**
a. Drop what you're doing to help her.
b. Agree to help if she'll give you candy.
c. Tell her to buzz off.

3 **Your sister has just got a really bad haircut. Do you . . . ?**
a. Tell her that her smile looks brighter now.
b. Buy her a hat.
c. Take her picture and post it all over the Internet.

4 **Your sister has just got a bad grade on her report card. Do yo**
a. Offer to tutor her.
b. Tell her about the time you got a bad grade.
c. Race to be the first to tell a parent.

5 **Two of your sisters are in a fight. Do you . . . ?**
a. Call them into your room and help them solve their problem.
b. Ignore them and read a book.
c. Say bad stuff about each sister to make them more angry.

6 **Your sister wants to borrow money. Do you . . . ?**
a. Lend it to her and trust her to pay you back.
b. Write out an I.O.U. and make her sign it in blood.
c. Tell her to go and print her own money.

7 **You and your sister both want to run for school president. Do you . . . ?**
a. Offer to step aside because you know how much it means to her.
b. Say, "May the best person win."
c. Fake appendicitis so people feel sorry and vote for you.

8 **Someone at school is spreading mean gossip about your sister. Do you . . . ?**
a. Find out who started it and go with your sister to stick up for her.
b. Toilet-paper the person's locker.
c. Pretend it's Chinese whispers and add even juicier gossip to watch her squirm.

Give yourself 3 points for every a, 2 points for every b, and 1 point for every c.

20–24 points → *Congrats! You're a super sib!*
14–19 points → *Sorry—You're just a so-so sib.*
8–13 points → *You are one seriously lame sis; let's hope you have brothers!*

Why Can't I Write About Boston and Not Boring-Old Oregon?
by Joey Reel

Top five reasons I want to go to Boston someday:

1. To see the real <u>Little</u> <u>Women</u> house
2. To see the real <u>Little</u> <u>Women</u> house
3. To see the real <u>Little</u> <u>Women</u> house
4. To see the real <u>Little</u> <u>Women</u> house
5. To see the real <u>Little</u> <u>Women</u> house

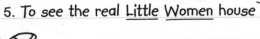

747 = Kind of plane I would fly to Boston

399 = address of Louisa May Alcott's house, Orchard House, on Lexington Road, Concord, near Boston, where she wrote <u>Little</u> <u>Women</u>

12 = acres of apples trees at Orchard House in Concord

7 = number of rooms in Louisa's house you can actually see online

$9.95 = cost of <u>Little</u> <u>Women</u> journal with pen, pencil, and ruler at gift shop

17 = number of times I have looked it up

400 = number of pictures I would take of Orchard House, where <u>Little</u> <u>Women</u> takes place

0 = number of times I get to go

3 million = number of times Joey has said "Boston" in the past two weeks ~S

Nah-uh! —J

Once Upon a Bad Hair Day

Saturday morning

7:36

I woke up and thought, *Today's the day! The day of the cake-off!*

Then I remembered I was mad at Alex. I yanked the covers over my head. Curled up. Fell back to sleep.

8:36

I overslept! I woke up to what sounded like a lawn mower (or was it a bulldozer?) right outside my door. Either way, it sounded like somebody was about to bulldoze the house down. When I padded out into the hall, I realized it was just Alex and her blow-dryer.

8:39

Downstairs in kitchen. I popped a blueberry Toasty Pop into the toaster. I stuck my tongue out at my toaster-reflection, which looked like somebody who had been up half the night icing cupcakes and hadn't bothered to brush her hair yet.

8:42

On the table, I found a shiny cupcake tin with a red ribbon around it. It was not from the charity shop. It was not from Oxfam. It was not from some old-lady garage sale. It was *brand-spanking-new,* shinier than a toaster, and the cupcake hollows were filled with cake-decorating stuff—edible glitter, sparkle gel (looks like glitter-glue but you can eat it), even a pack of sugar-dusted rubber duckies made of icing.

Up popped my blueberry strudel. Toaster Girl was smiling now.

Mom walked in. "Mom? Is this for me?" I ran over and hugged her. "I love it! I can put some finishing touches on my cake, and use the little rubber duckies like mini moat swimmers around my castle!"

"I know it's last minute—but I had a gift certificate

from work and I just thought you should have a few fun things to use for the cake-off. I'm so disappointed I can't be there today, Stevie. I wasn't counting on having to reshoot my Apple Slump segment. I guess the apples slumped a bit more than they were supposed to." I laughed.

"I know you'll do great, sweetie. Just remember, have fun."

"I will."

As Mom and I discussed plans for the day, I found myself dreaming of sugar-dusted rubber duckies bobbing on a moat of blue sprinkles.

9:09

Final dress rehearsal today. It turned out to be a good thing after all that I wasn't a princess in the play. I don't think I could handle the stress of wearing such a complicated costume. There were like seventeen pieces to the princess dress, and Alex could only find eleven of them.

She was acting normal to me, as if nothing had happened yesterday. Then I remembered — she didn't even know that I had talked to Mr. Cannon. She was way too busy rushing around like a chicken in a rainstorm—darting from mirror to mirror, flinging velvety, satiny, lacy pantaloon-type clothing around all over the upstairs.

Anger bubbled to the surface again, flaring inside me like a hot flame. I guess no amount of cupcakes could put out that fire.

9:11

P.U. Alex was combing goopy, gross, smelly stuff into her hair, and it was making my eyes smart and stinking up the whole entire house.

"Greasy grimy gopher guts!" Joey said, pinching her nose and scrunching up her face.

I, for one, agreed.

"Something is rotten in the state of Delaware," said Joey.

"Denmark," said Alex.

"What's with the smelly stuff?" Joey asked.

"You mean thou odiferous stench?" I asked, tossing in some Shakespeare, too. "Foh! Prithee, stand away. 'Tis the rankest compound of villainous smell that ever offended nostril."

Alex, Queen of Shakespeare, rolled her eyes at us. "It's to make my hair straight!" she informed us. "But it's not working."

"Why do you need your hair straight?" Joey asked. My question exactly.

"I'm *Princess Winnifred*," Alex said, like that explained it. Joey and I shrugged. "Hello! You've seen the movie. The main princess does not have curly hair."

"She does so have curls," said Joey. "In the one where Carol Burnett is the queen."

"Well, I'm talking about the Broadway one with Sarah Jessica Parker. I looked it up online, and for your information, Sarah Jessica Parker definitely does not have curls. Her hair is really long, almost to her waist—even longer than yours, Joey—and she has a long, tiny braid down one side."

"Dare to be different," I told my sister.

"I can't. Zoe DuFranc is Larken, and she has dark curly hair, and we'll look too much alike."

"Well, you smell like an art project," I snapped.

"And you look like a mop of wet spaghetti!" said Joey.

9:30

Dad suggested that Alex try sleeping with orange-juice cans in her hair (for curlers). The bigger the curler, the straighter the hair.

As much as I'd like to see Alex with orange-juice-can hair, she didn't have time to sleep. The dress rehearsal was starting in a few hours.

"You could press your hair in the dictionary," I told her. "Like we used to do with violets."

"C'mon, Stevie, you have to help me."

"Why me? What about Joey?"

"Don't look at me," said Joey. "Dad's taking me to the Cascades Playhouse to check out their magic flying carpet."

"Well, don't look at me. I've got to get ready for the cake-off."

"But your cake's made, isn't it? So you're ready."

"Don't you get it?" I practically bit her head off. My eyes flashed with fury. "This is a big day for me, too, you know. Yours is only a dress rehearsal, but mine is like, like the Cupcake *Olympics.*"

Alex just didn't get it. She didn't even seem to care that I was boiling mad. And to make things worse, by

189

the time I woke up this morning, my enchanted castle looked more like a slumped-over Tower of London.

"But you're not doing anything right this minute."

"Yes, I am! I'm waiting for Olivia to call. She's coming with me to the cake-off. Her mom's going to drive us."

"Well, I'm going with Scott and I'm going to be late—"

"Alex and Scott Towel, sittin' in a tree, K-I-S-S-I-N-G," sang Joey mockingly.

"Joey and Laurie, sittin' in a tree, K-I-S-S-I-N-G," I teased back, momentarily forgetting my anger.

"Laurie who?" Alex asked.

"You know. Laurie. The guy from *Little Women*. The one that likes Jo. Joey's in love with him."

"So? Alex is in love with Scott Towel and that Voice Man guy."

"Let's go, Joey!" Dad called up the stairs.

"I'm leaving, too. Good luck today, girls," said Mom.

"Alex, you're in charge," Dad reminded her.

Alex in charge of me?

"And I don't want to hear about any fighting," said Dad.

That shouldn't be hard. Since technically I still wasn't speaking to her.

9:37

Alex barged into my room, waving Mom's iron around. "Iron my hair!" she ordered me. She actually popped open the ironing board, laid her head down on it, and stretched out her long hair as if she were Rapunzel or something.

"You're joking, right?"

"No! Dad said Mom used to iron her hair in high school. C'mon! Hurry up!"

"No way am I going to iron your hair!" I protested.

"You have to," said Alex. "I'm in charge."

9:41

I had never ironed so much as a sock, much less my sister's hair!

If Alex knew how mad I was at her, she wouldn't let me near her hair with an iron… .

I got the iron really hot. Huffing and puffing. I must have accidentally set it on Puff the Magic Dragon, because hiccups of steam kept poofing out of the thing, even though I hadn't added a single drop of water. I started by ironing Alex's hair at the ends, about an inch at a time. Her hair is super-curly, and it took five minutes to iron one curl.

"Shouldn't I be using a towel or something to put over your hair?"

"Just iron!"

Alex muttered lines she was rehearsing while practically leaning upside-down on the ironing board.

"Hey! I think it's really working!" I said, surprised.

"Stop pressing the mist button," Alex ordered. *Ssssss!* Steam hissed off Alex's hair, sending up cumulus-cloud puffs, like smoke signals.

I couldn't help cracking up. "You look like one of those cartoon characters that are mad and have steam coming out of their ears."

"As long as I look like a *straight-haired* cartoon," she snapped.

9:45

Operation Straight Hair was going great, until ... the phone rang.

Olivia! I grabbed the cordless, switching the iron to my left hand.

"Stevie!" Alex said, annoyed.

"Don't worry. I've got it. Just hold still. DO NOT move a hair."

It was Olivia. Even though I was going to see my best friend in about twenty-one minutes, she started yakking away about all this stuff that happened yesterday since I'd seen her, telling me all about:

- A spitball catapult some kid named Dylan built in carpentry
- How she fell asleep studying the night before and messed up Potamia (as in flubbed her test on Ancient Mesopotamia)
- Her new piano teacher's hairy-toed bare feet (Hairy Feet wears flip-flops!)

9:49

"What's that burning smell?" Alex asked.

All of a sudden, I smelled a stinking smell. An awful smell. A terrible, horrible *burning* smell, vile and odiferous. Worse than the Chinese Fried Rice Incident—

the time I burned the rice in a saucepan so bad it filled the whole kitchen with smoke.

Holy Hamlet! Alex's hair!

I dropped the phone.

9:51

Alex yanked her hair out from under the iron. The iron and ironing board went crashing to the floor. I grabbed the iron, turning it off before it could burn anything else.

The back of her hair was ... smoking! Way worse than a cartoon character.

Alex stood up.

All of a sudden, to my horror, I saw a big hunk of Alex's beautiful, once-curly long hair fall to the ground. Then another. I'd left the iron on her hair too long!

Alex turned around.

The shape of the iron, like a big triangle, was burned out of the back of her hair.

"Uh!" I sucked in a horrified breath, my mouth gaping open. I covered my mouth with both hands, not daring to say a word.

"Look at me! My hair! And the play is tomorrow!

What am I going to do?" She shook a fistful of burned hair at me. "You could have burned me *and* this old house down!"

Alex zinged from mirror to mirror. In the bathroom, under the bright lights, she held up a hand mirror to inspect the back of her hair.

"*Ahhhhh!* Look what you've done to me!" she yelled (and a bunch of other not-so-polite stuff. I think "canker blossom" and "be-slubbering fly-bitten rat's bane" were in there somewhere). "I look like a scarecrow!"

"Too bad the play isn't *The Wizard of Oz!*" I said, trying to lighten the mood, but it didn't exactly go down well.

Alex shook the hand mirror at me accusingly. "You did this on purpose, Stevie Reel! Don't think I don't know—"

"I did not! It was an accident! I was talking to Livvie and not paying attention for like one second. I didn't do anything on purpose. You're the one who had to iron your stupid hair."

"Oh, yeah? You're just jealous."

"Me, jealous? Ha!"

"You know you've been dying to get back at me ever since I got the lead and you didn't."

"And whose fault is that? I didn't even stand a chance, because you went running to Mr. Cannon, telling him that I was too busy and shouldn't get the lead."

If I had thrown a rock at Alex and hit her right between the eyes, I don't think I could have stunned her any more. For once, my sister wasn't acting.

Silence fell between us, thick and impenetrable, like a curtain that drops, separating actor from audience.

When I finally worked up the courage to look up at my sister and meet her eyes, I saw that they weren't hard anymore. In fact, it was impossible to stay screaming-mad at somebody who looked so pathetic, standing there in her pajama top and princess pantaloons, with her hair sticking up like an inside-out umbrella.

"You know about that?" she half whispered.

Just then, I heard a car honk outside. The doorbell rang. Olivia! It was time for the cake-off.

Before either of us could say another word, I was on my way out the door, teetering down the sidewalk, trying not to topple my castle.

Off with Her Hair!
by Joey Reel

Good news: As soon as Dad and I got home from the Playhouse, we got Alex to stop crying.

Bad news: She looked like a cross between Einstein and a Monkee, with puffy raccoon eyes from crying.

Good news: The Hair Place said they could fix Alex's hair before the dress rehearsal!

Bad news: They'd have to cut her hair, really short.

Good news: Alex could play Prince Dauntless, instead of Princess Winnifred.

Bad news: Alex did not find that one teensy bit funny.

← Prince Dauntless

Good news: I thought it was pretty hilarious, and
I knew Stevie would, too.

Bad news: She'd have to wear a wig now, for
the play.

Good news: Short hair fits really well
under a wig!

Bad news: Dad said our princess wig
has moth holes.

Good news: Alex was sure to win first prize in the
International Bad Hair Hall of Fame.

Bad news: Alex didn't want to win anything — she
just wanted her hair back.

Good news: Stevie measured my hair last night,
and it was ten inches long! Finally!

Bad news: So I had to give all my hair away.

Good news: I did it! I CUT OFF MY HAIR!
Just like Jo.

Bad news: I look like a boy.
Just like Jo.

Good news: I donated my ten-inch (!) ponytail to Locks of Love to make wigs for kids who have cancer. Kind of like Jo. But more like Beth, who always gave stuff to poor people.

Bad news: My ears stick out now, and did I mention ... I look like a boy!

Things that are OK to iron:
- Wrinkly clothes from under your bed
- Recycled wrapping paper (on low!)
- Crayons (between waxed paper for making stained-glass pictures)
- Homework chewed by the dog

Things that are NOT OK to iron:

- Your shirt while it's still on you
- Waffles (unless it's a waffle iron)
- The dog's tail
- YOUR SISTER'S HAIR!

Tips if you want curly hair:

- Go to bed with wet hair.
- Do not wash hair every day.
- Eat bread crusts (or is it carrots?).
- Move to Florida (humidity factor).
- Leave braids in hair for about a week.

Tips if you want straight hair:

- Use orange-juice cans for curlers.
- Press hair in dictionary.
- Buy stock in hair spray (P.U.!).
- ~~Elmer's glue~~
- Stand in front of fan (or lean out car window).
- DO NOT IRON!

The Unhaired Sisters

5:19

I came home from the cake-off to a house full of short-haired strangers (a.k.a. Alex AND Joey!).

"Your hair," I blurted in surprise, then covered my mouth.

"I know," said Alex. "It's shorter than Shakespeare's."

"But you're not as bald as Humpty Dumpty!" Joey added encouragingly.

My sister reached up and tugged a short hunk of hair over her ears, as if yanking on it might somehow make it longer.

Joey jumped in. "It's just like the Great Tragedy in *Little Women*!"

"How is this like Beth dying?" I asked impatiently.

"No, it's like the time Jo tried to curl Meg's hair, and she burned off all the ends."

"This *is* a Great Tragedy," said Alex, tragically touching her short mop of curls. She went on to tell us about the dress rehearsal I'd missed, and the fact that her moth-munched wig fell off no less than seven times during rehearsal.

Then Joey told us about coming home and finding Einstein Alex and getting her hair chopped off and giving it to Locks of Love.

"How does it feel?" I asked.

"Weird," said Joey. "It was scary at first, but then *thrilling*."

"Thrilling, huh?"

"You know. Just like when Jo March cut off all her hair and sold it for twenty-five dollars to help her family because they were so poor."

"That was a brave thing you did, Duck," I told her.

"Stop calling me Duck. Call me Jo!"

"And way generous." I felt guilty, twirling a lock of my own long hair.

"Yeah, but then on the way home, at the super-market, a guy stepped on my foot by mistake, and his wife said, 'Say you're sorry to the boy.' Try explaining that I'm a girl named Joey with *this* hair," Joey said.

At least she could laugh about it. "Now we'll have to call you J-O-E instead of just J-O," I teased her.

Mom and Dad came in. "Tell us all about the cake-off," said Mom.

"They must have loved your enchanted castle," Dad said.

"Did you win a blue ribbon?" Joey asked eagerly.

"Nope."

"Did you win a gold ribbon?"

"Nope."

"Did you win a red or green or purple or silver?"

"Nope. No ribbons, Joe. Although I could have won the You're-the-Only-Person-Here-Under-Fifty ribbon."

Mom and Dad laughed. Alex went to check her hair in the bathroom mirror for the hundredth time since I'd walked in the door.

"I'm not kidding, you guys. You've never seen such fancy cakes in your life. There was a candy-cane cake, a cake called Red Velvet, and a daffodil cake. Every ingredient in the whole entire cake was yellow, and it was decorated with tons of real daffodils."

"That sounds pretty," said Mom. "I'm sorry I missed that."

"But your castle was so great," Joey said. "How come you didn't win anything? Too many I-Hate-My-Sister cupcakes?"

I glanced towards the bathroom, hoping Alex hadn't heard. "No-way," I said, making my "no" sound like it had two syllables. "I'm not kidding, these people are so way good, like professionals. When they saw my castle, since it's made of cupcakes, I had to enter in the Sculpture Cake division. They had cakes like a pyramid, a dog in his doghouse, a stack of books, and a snowman cake. There was even a cake that looked like a big giant bloodshot eyeball."

"Did you know Shakespeare invented the word *eyeball*?" Dad asked.

"But I bet he didn't invent eyeball *cake*," said Joey.

"He also invented the word *unhair*," said Mom, grinning.

"As in, 'Unhair me, you villain!'" I waved my arm around in a fake sword-fight.

Joey flipped to the back of the big dictionary. "It's in here. It's a real word. 'To deprive of hair.'"

"I can use it in a sentence. My *unhaired* sisters look really weird," I teased.

"I heard that," said Alex, still tugging on her hair as she came back into the room.

"So what cake won the contest?" said Joey.

"The Seattle Space Needle cake won first prize. I think maybe they cheated, though. Because how do you get a big round UFO-shaped cake to balance on top of little skinny legs? They would've had to use wires or pipe cleaners or something, and that's against the rules."

"No fair," said Joey. "I think you should have won the Most-Blue-Sprinkles-on-a -Cake-Ever Award."

Alex lifted up her flip-flop and showed off the bottom, which was dotted with blue sprinkles!

"Oops," I said.

"Well, there's always next year," said Dad.

"And you still have the play," said Joey.

"And I still have my hair," I joked.

Everybody (minus Alex) laughed.

THE SHOW MUST GO ON
Starring Alex

Me: *(Riding in car on the way to the play.)* I can't believe it's opening day.

Stevie: I know. I'm so excited. Seems like we've been practicing forever. *Me-may-mah-mo-moo. (Does voice warm-up.)*

Me: No, I mean, I can't believe I have to go out there, like this. *(Tugs on short hair.)* I asked Mr. Cannon yesterday if he thought we could postpone the first show, since it's only a Sunday matinee.

Dad: *(From front seat.)* What did he say?

Me: He said short hair was not really a good enough reason to cancel the show.

Dad: *(Coughs. Clears throat.)*

Mom: *(Muffles laugh.)* I think Mr. Cannon's right, honey.

Me: They might as well just call me Princess Baldo instead of Winnifred.

Joey: Princess Baldo! Good one.

Stevie: I don't see why you're so upset.

Who's going to know? You'll be wearing
a wig.

Joey: Yeah, you can't even see the moth
balls.

Stevie: Moth *holes.*

Dad: Your sisters are right. That's what
makes a play exciting. You never know
what's going to happen, and you just have
to improvise.

Me: It's not just the wig... I don't know.
There's just something about everything
that's happened. It's like bad luck. Like
the play is cursed or something.

Joey: Ooh! Ooh! It's like that curse Dad told
us about. You know, the Macbeth curse!

Me: *(Groaning.)* Joey! Don't say "Macbeth"!

Joey: It doesn't matter in the car. It's only
if somebody says "Macbeth" in the theater
before the play, right, Dad?

Stevie: *(Teasing.)* But what if the play's
Macbeth?

Me: *(Growling, putting hands over ears.)*
Stop saying "MACBETH," everybody!

Joey: *(Practically bouncing up and down.)* And if you do say "Macbeth," you have to go outside the building, spin around three times, spit, then curse, and knock on the door till they let you back in. That's so cool!

Mom: Alex, it's just an old superstition. Dad was just telling Joey for fun.

Me: *(Glancing over at Stevie.)* I just don't feel right. Something isn't right. It's like I shouldn't even go onstage or something. I don't know. I have a bad feeling.

Dad: It's called opening-day jitters. I used to have to go backstage and huff and puff into a paper bag just to calm myself down. And Mom used to sing "Mary Had a Little Lamb" to steady her nerves.

Mom: *(Shrugging.)* Whatever works.

Stevie: Alex has stage fright? And I don't?

Me: *(Clutching stomach.)* I think I'm going to be sick. Can somebody open a window, please?

Stevie and Joey: *(Move over to one side, away from me.)*

Me: You don't know, Stevie. You weren't there for dress rehearsal yesterday. A bunch of stuff went wrong. And I messed up "Happily Ever After."

Dad: You know, they say if you have a bad dress rehearsal, that means good luck for opening day.

Joey: Does that work for plays besides *Macbeth*?

Me: *(Sinking back into seat.)* That does it. I'm cursed for sure.

Mattresses and Mishaps
Or How I Know Alex's Play Is Cursed
by Joey Reel

1. Some kid announced, "The play you are about to see is called <u>Once</u> <u>Upon</u> <u>a</u> <u>Buttress</u>." Ha!

2. One of the knights couldn't find the weights for Princess Winnie to lift, so he brought out a broom, and it nearly knocked the prince's eye out.

3. The band director played the wrong music for "Spanish Panic," so everybody was in a not-Spanish panic.

4. The fire alarm went off during "Many Moons Ago" because of the fog machine.

5. The Wizard conjured up a banana, then ate it, but he left the banana peel and Prince Dauntless slipped on it for real!

6. Some kid playing the Minstrel lost his voice and had to trade places with the guy who plays the King (who's mute). Double ha!

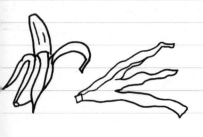

RING!

7. A piece of the set fell on the Minstrel (who used to be king).
8. Alex played Winnifred without a wig (in short hair!), screwed up a bunch of her lines, and blanked on one whole verse of "Swamps of Home." (Stevie had to sing Alex's lines and pretend that's what was supposed to happen.)

And that was just Act I!

Ouch!

The Curtain Falls

During intermission, I came out into the audience to say hi to Livvie and her parents, then ran over to find Mom, Dad, and Joey.

Everybody started talking at once. Dad was giving me tips, Mom was telling me how great my voice sounded on my solo parts, and Joey and I were cracking up over all the crazy stuff that had happened in Act One.

Just then, Scott Towel came up behind me. "Hey, Steven," he said, tapping me on the back. "You've got to do something. Quick. It's a disaster." He pointed in the direction of the stage.

"It's the curse!" said Joey.

"It's not that bad," I told him. "I know a lot of stuff

went wrong, but at least the audience was laughing."

"No, I mean Alex. You know how she messed up the first act?"

"Hey, I tried to save her that time she went blank and her voice locked up."

"Well, now she's locked *herself* up in the dressing room backstage, and she says she's not coming out."

"We have a dressing room? And it locks?"

"OK, the props closet or whatever. Behind the stage. It's like she has stage fright or something. It's not like her," Scott Towel said.

"She's probably still upset about her hair disaster. She'll get over it."

"No. I mean it. She's *really* not coming out."

"She can't not come out. The play starts again in less than fifteen minutes."

"Exactly. You've got to go and talk to her."

"Like I told her, it's just opening-day jitters," said Dad. "I'd better go and see if there's anything I can do."

"No. It's OK, Dad. Let me." I had a feeling I knew what was freaking her out. And it wasn't the short hair. Or stage fright. Or some stupid curse.

TALE OF TWO SISTERS
Starring Alex

Me: *(Sitting on top of a guitar case in the supply closet. Suddenly, hears a knock at the door.)* Scott?

Stevie: Hey. It's me. Stevie.

Me: *(Goes over and puts ear to door.)*

Stevie: C'mon, Alex. You've got to come out of there.

Me: *(No, I don't.)*

Stevie: Alex, just open the door. I have something I want to give you.

Me: *(No way am I opening this door.)*

Stevie: I know you can hear me, Alex. Alex? Look, I've talked to your door at home plenty of times. I'm pretty good at it even. So if you think I'm going away, I'm not. *(Sound of Stevie sliding to floor.)*

Me: *(Silence. A minute goes by. Say something!)* Are you still there?

Stevie: I'm right here, Alex.

Me: *(More silence.)*

Stevie: Can't you just talk to me? What's wrong? Is it that you think you've messed up the play? It's not that bad. Really. It's just a matinee, mostly for little kids. People thought it was funny. Honest.

Me: Not just the play. I've messed up a lot of things. You. Us.

Stevie: *(Silence.)*

Me: All I could think about was wanting the part so bad, and now I've got it, but I feel miserable, and I'm not even doing a good job and then you step in and save me *again,* and you did a better job than me, and I'm supposed to be the actor.

Stevie: Alex ...

Me: I should never have got the part, Stevie.

Stevie: What do you mean? Of course you should have.

Me: No, you don't understand. I did a terrible thing. I was mean, and selfish—I just

wanted the part so bad, that's all I
could see, and now, every time I think
about what I did, it makes me want to
throw up.

Stevie: You mean about what you said
to Mr. Cannon?

Me: I'm sorry, Stevie. I really let you down.
And I let myself down, too. It shouldn't
have freaked me out that you wanted to
be in the play. I should have been
happy that we *both* could be in the play
together.

Stevie: *(Silence.)*

Me: So now you know why I can't go back
out there. How can I look anybody
in the face? Mom or Dad or Joey or
the audience ... And now I have raccoon
eyes again from crying and I feel
like I'm going to throw up every time
I try to sing. Not to mention, I hate
my hair!

Stevie: Well, I, for one, wouldn't mind
seeing those raccoon eyes.

Me: I'm sorry, Stevie. I'm so, so sorry. Can you ever—

Stevie: That's all I wanted to hear you say. That you're sorry.

Me: So, you're not mad at me?

Stevie: Nope. Not anymore. I took that out on a few dozen cupcakes. I mean, OK, it did hurt my feelings that you'd say something on purpose that could hurt my chances of getting the lead. But let's face it—that's not why Mr. Cannon didn't pick me. He didn't pick me because he wanted to pick you. Alex.

Me: Are you sure?

Stevie: Mr. C said from the beginning that he needed me in the chorus, and I think he meant it.

Me: *(Sniffling.)* Really?

Stevie: Yeah. And I'm OK with that. Of course, burning your hair not-on-purpose did help me feel a little better. *(Laughs awkwardly.)*

Me: You mean you forgive me?

Stevie: You forgive me for burning your
  hair totally-by-accident, right? Hey.
  You're my sister.

(Click. Door opens!)

*(Stevie opens hand, holds out missing
Comedy charm, and presses it into my palm,
just before Act 2.)*

In the Pink

I was singing "Happily Ever After" from *Once Upon a Mattress* as I swirled a ruby-slipper-red ribbon of fruit into the batter, mixing up a brand-new batch of cupcakes. Vanilla-raspberry-swirl batter with light pink fluffy icing.

I stopped mixing to line each space in the muffin tin with a different cupcake liner. Shiny gold foil for Alex like a princess crown, smiley faces for Jo/Joey, G clefs and musical notes for me.

"More cupcakes?" Mom asked, coming into the kitchen. "They sure smell good." She looked surprised when she saw the fluffy pink icing I was whipping up. Baby pink. Bubble-gum pink. Princess-not-porcupine pink.

"This is new," she remarked, reaching a finger into the bowl. I didn't even bother to swat away her hand today.

"What do you think?" I asked.

"Heaven," said Mom.

"Well, I'm going to call them Pink Velvet. Like Red Velvet, only pink. With my special secret ingredient." I showed Mom all the crazy cupcake liners I'd found at this store with Olivia. "I'm going to make individual ones for Alex and Joey and you and Dad and everybody. Each one will have its own personality."

Mom pointed to the tin that had already come out of the oven. "I think this one has a split personality," Mom said, picking up the cracked-in-half cupcake.

"You can have that one," I said, laughing.

Mom took a bite as I began to ice the cupcake for Alex. Using a fine tip from my cake-decorating set, I squeezed out a fancy letter *A* onto the pink icing, and dotted it with candy silver pearls.

"Stevie, these are really remarkable. Mmm. I thought maybe you'd be out of the cupcake craze now that the cake-off's over."

"No way. Making cupcakes puts me in a good mood. See, whatever I'm feeling, I put it into the cupcakes."

"Like the I-Hate-My-Sister cupcakes I heard Joey mention?" Mom said in her disapproving tone.

"Joey, who, wha?" said my little sister, following her nose into the kitchen.

"Just in time, Duck. You can help choose what you want on your special cupcake. I have candy hearts."

"Did you girls know that candy hearts with sayings have been around—"

"Since you were a girl!" Joey and I said at the same time.

Mom laughed. "I was going to say since the Civil War, thank you very much."

"Same difference," said Joey, and we both cracked up again.

Joey fingered her way through candy heart sayings, reading off GO FISH, HEART OF GOLD, QUEEN BEE. She handed me three that said UR A QT.

Joey looked at the pink fluffy icing, dotted with flowers and hearts and rainbows. "These look different. Not like the mad ones you've been making lately. These are almost happy!"

221

"These are more like Make-Up-with-My-Sister cupcakes. The other ones were more like Break-Up cupcakes, when Alex and I were mad and fighting. It's OK to bake cupcakes when you're in a good mood, too, you know. Cupcakes make people happy. It's like a rule."

"Stevie, is this what you've been doing all along?" Mom asked. "Not just stockpiling cupcakes for the cake-off, but baking to deal with your feelings?"

"Stevie always bakes cupcakes when she's mad," said Joey.

"I guess so," I said. "It's not like I planned it. But it works. You guys put feelings into acting. I put them into baking cupcakes."

"Like the My-Sister-Is-a-Porcupine cupcakes and the I-Burned-My-Sister's-Hair-and-Feel-Bad cupcakes," said Joey.

"Mmm-mmm." Mom made more yummy sounds, but she had a stare-at-the-toaster, Fondue-Sue look on her face at the same time. "Stevie?" said Mom, polishing off the last of the icing on her finger. "Any chance you could finish decorating these later?"

"Huh?"

"And come with me?"

"Why? Where are we going?"

"To the studio. Grab a jacket. You, my brilliant middle daughter, have just given me a genius of an idea."

I made a funny face at Joey, but she didn't notice. She had her nose too far into the icing bowl. "Don't eat all the icing!" I called over my shoulder, as Fondue Sue grabbed me by the hand and herded me out of the kitchen.

Joey's Oregon State Poem
by Joey Reel

The I Wanna Go to Boston Blues

I wanna go to Boston someday
But I promise
To read a Beverly Cleary book
And watch <u>The</u> <u>Simpsons</u>
Before I go.

I wanna go to Boston someday
But I promise
To search for a thunder egg,
Call my sister a hairy triton,
And eat a hazelnut
Before I go.

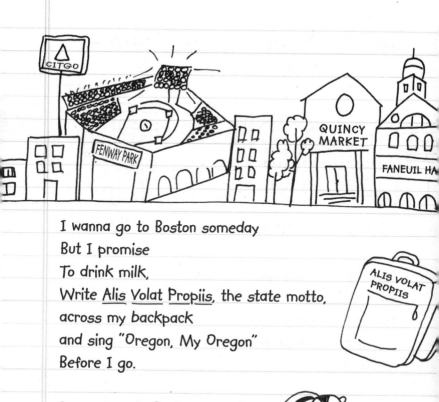

I wanna go to Boston someday
But I promise
To drink milk,
Write <u>Alis</u> <u>Volat</u> <u>Propiis</u>, the state motto,
across my backpack
and sing "Oregon, My Oregon"
Before I go.

I wanna go to Boston someday
But I promise
To hug a beaver (stuffed-animal chipmunk?)
First thing
Just as soon as I get home
From Louisa May's house.
Someday.

Over the Moon

Mom asked me to wait outside the program manager's office. I couldn't figure out why she'd dragged me all the way down here just to sit and watch her through the window arguing with her boss.

Actually, I couldn't quite tell if all the waving of arms meant that she was excited or frustrated. The last time I'd been at Mom's studio was when I'd blurted out about wanting to audition for the play. That's when my fight with Alex started. It seemed like forever ago now that we'd made up and the play was over.

I found myself there again, flipping through old magazines. In the middle of some women's magazine, something caught my eye: an ad for moisturizing lotion with a French-sounding name.

"From the French phrase *bien dans sa peau,* which means to be happy in your own skin."

Happy in your own skin.

The words jumped off the page at me, making my heart skip. Maybe I had been trying too hard to do the things Alex does. Wanting to act in plays, stealing her shirt, going out for the same role.

Even though I think it's never a bad thing to take a risk and try something new, I wasn't Alex. I would never be Alex. I didn't even want to be Alex.

I was Me. Myself. I.

Stevie.

Happy in my own skin.

Or as the Bard himself said: "To thine own self be true."

Being true to myself was singing—using my voice to sing in the play. And already making plans for next year's cake-off: world's biggest cupcake!

Who knew that moisturizer held the secret of life?

I'd almost forgotten about Mom when she tapped on the glass and waved me into the office.

"Hi, honey, c'mon in. You remember Betsy. Betsy,

this is my middle daughter, Stevie." Mom hooked a hunk of hair behind her ear, pushing it back into place. "Stevie, I pitched an idea to Betsy for our next show, and she's agreed to go to the station manager on the strength of the idea and push for more episodes of *Fondue Sue* next season. Now, you tell me, isn't that just *fan*tastic?"

"Yeah, Mom, that's great!" I tried to sound as happy as Mom even though I still didn't have a clue what that had to do with me.

"It'll be all about baking as a way of channeling your feelings and emotions," said Betsy. "Your mom's been telling me about all your cupcakes."

"Hey, yeah! That's a great idea for a show, Mom."

"Maybe we can even think of a way to make them healthy," said Betsy. "You know, like, courgette cupcakes or carrot-cake cupcakes."

I exchanged glances with Mom, trying not to laugh.

"And that's not all," said Mom. "Betsy had another brilliant idea." Mom nodded towards her boss.

"I was thinking, if you'd be willing, how would you like to come on the show with your mom, help her do some baking, maybe talk a little bit about your cupcakes? What do you think?"

"Me? On TV? Are you serious?"

"I think it would be great," Betsy said. "Help us reach out to a younger demographic. Get kids interested in cooking and baking."

It was all I could do to keep from jumping in the air, throwing my arms out, and screaming YAY!

"Honey, isn't this exciting?" Mom said, squeezing me in a sideways hug.

I had to leave Mom and Betsy to work out some of the details with the station manager. Inside, I was turning somersaults as I walked back out into the hall. I tried to steady myself by staring at animal pictures in *National Geographic*. I even tried solving a *Reader's Digest* crossword puzzle.

Seven down. Expression of high joy. Eleven letters. OVERTHEMOON.

"Mom?" I asked, when she was finally done and we got back into the car. "Do you mind if—could we make a stop on the way home?"

Holy Hamlet!

"No way!" shrieked Alex.

"Then what happened?" Joey asked.

Alex, Joey and I were all three sitting cross-legged on my bed, and I, Yours Truly, had called a meeting of the Sisters Club. After our secret handshake, I told my sisters all about Mom dragging me to the studio and barging into the program manager's office and blurting out her Big Idea. I still had my hoodie on, pulled tight around my face, and I hadn't yet breathed a word about an even bigger surprise still to come.

"I've never seen Mom talk so fast," I told my sisters. "We're talking spit flying."

"Ooh," said Joey, wiping her face like it was happening right then.

"So, go on," Alex coaxed.

"Mom told her boss that her daughter *(moi)* had given her a wonderful idea, and that they should do a whole show on cooking with emotion, you know, like baking stuff when you feel lousy or happy or just plain blue. She explained that I've been making these I-Hate-My-Sister cupcakes and everything—sorry, Alex!—and how she'd like to do a show about channeling your feelings and stuff through cooking and baking."

"So, hurry up, tell us, what did the Big Boss say?"

For a second, I could hardly breathe, being back with my sisters, having a meeting of the Sisters Club, like old times.

"So Betsy, Mom's boss, she had to clear it with the station manager, Mr. Morrissey, and he came over and went like this." In a deep, sort of scary voice, I said, "'I don't like it, Susan. I *love* it!'"

"Aaah!" Joey squealed and Alex clapped her hands together.

"Wait, that's not all," I said, trying to eke out the suspense. "Mom morphed into this other person and said, 'Let's talk turkey, Nolan,' and I thought she meant a show about turkey, you know, like for Thanksgiving, but then I got it that she meant money, because next thing I knew I was back out in the hall reading about meerkats in a ripped-up *National Geographic*."

"I love meerkats!" said Joey.

"So there I was, reading all about meerkat super-families and thinking how these guys were so cool. I learned that their life span is only like ten years and just when I was getting bummed out thinking that if I were a meerkat, I would be, well—let's face it—dead, Mom came out and hugged me. l mean, lifted me up off the floor and told me they'd renewed her show for thirteen more episodes!"

More squealing from Alex and Joey.

"And …" I waited for them to calm down. "AND … here I was, picturing myself in Meerkat Heaven, when the Big Boss said, 'Stevie, how would you like to be on TV? Betsy's told me her idea and we'd love for you to come on the show. After all, you were the inspiration.'"

My sisters jumped up and down and hugged each other and Joey said, "Amazingness!"

Alex made a poor-me face and fake-whined, "I'm so jealous!"

"Yeah, I know it's cool and everything, but just think of the stage fright!" I squealed. "I mean, it's TV!"

"Don't worry," Alex said, brushing my fringe to the side. "I can give you some acting tips so you won't hurl in front of a live studio audience or anything." Joey and I laughed, and Alex smiled, her eyes flashing in a happy-for-me kind of way, not a green-eyed-monster kind of way.

All of a sudden, I sprang up off the bed and rooted through a jumble of clothes in my bottom drawer. I pulled out the black shirt I'd worn for the audition. "Here's your black shirt, by the way," I said, giving it back to Alex.

"Aren't you ever going to take your coat off and stay awhile?" Joey asked, eyeing my laced-up hoodie.

I took a deep breath and loosened the ties around my hood. "Ta-da!" I said, tossing back my hood and revealing my surprise.

"Holy Hamlet!" Alex shrieked when she saw my hair.

"Leaping Lady Macbeth!" Joey said, sucking in a breath. She held one hand over her mouth while she pointed at my head with the other.

"Your hair! You cut off your hair?!" Alex shrieked again. "It's shorter than Shakespeare's! Shorter than Hamlet's!"

"But you're not as bald as Humpty Dumpty," said Joey, giggling.

"Look who's talking!" I said, and all three of us cracked up.

"Who unhaired you?" Joey asked.

"Yeah, when did this happen?" asked Alex.

"On the way home," I said.

My sisters circled around me, like I was the bride at a wedding or whatever, inspecting me from all sides.

"'As she spoke, Jo'—I mean Stevie—'took off her bonnet, and a general outcry arose,'" Joey said, reciting lines from her beloved Chapter 15, "'for all her abundant hair was cut short.'"

"That bad, huh?" I asked. "Do I look like an elf?"

"No," said Alex. "It's sassy-chic. Makes you look older."

"And your ears don't even stick out," said Joey.

Real vs. Reel Hair Disasters
by Joey Reel

Famous hair disasters:
- Cruella de Vil
- Madame Pomp-E-Doo
  (Alex said it's Pompadour)
- Cleopatra
- Marie Antoinette
- Bride of Frankenstein
- Humpty Dumpty (famous no-hair disaster!)

Reel family hair disasters:
- Mom's first dance
- Dad in <u>King Lear</u>
- Alex as Rapunzel (her hair got stuck on fake thorn bushes)
- My bald spot (when I hit my head and they shaved it)
- Larry Lion (when I dropped Alex's stuffed lion in the mud and cut off his mane)
  - FrankenStevie (on Halloween)

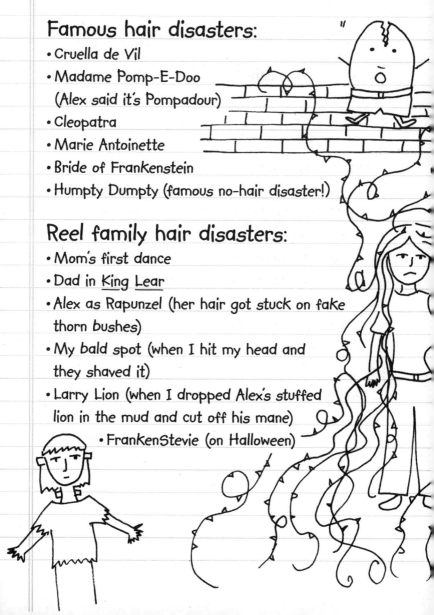

Happily Ever After

Once my sisters and I had recovered from Short Hair Shock, we realized we still had the rest of the day together without a play or a practice or a cake-off. Alex, Joey, and I sat on the floor in the family room, watching the video Dad had taken of *Once Upon a Mattress,* and laughing our heads off.

"Wait. Back it up, back it up," said Joey. "I've got to see that prince guy slip on the banana peel again."

"I can't believe that wasn't actually on purpose," I said.

"Good thing everybody thought it was, though," said Alex.

We watched the whole thing, reciting lines and singing along with the songs. And the parts where stuff went wrong—we watched those at least three times each.

"Read again what they said in the review," said Alex.

I grabbed the sheets I had printed off the school website and read aloud. "'It's a tragedy that more people did not turn out to see the musical comedy *Once Upon a Mattress*.'"

"Just skip to the good parts," said Joey.

"OK, OK. Here we go. 'Despite a few stumbles in the first half, the cast of *Once Upon a Mattress* cleverly turned these mishaps to their advantage, adding funny moments with comic timing that could not have been better had they been rehearsed.'

"Here's my favorite part. 'One such move had Stevie Reel, sister to Alex, the play's lead, stepping out of the chorus to fill in the lyrics on "Happily Ever After" with her singular, silver-tongued voice.'"

"Where do they get this stuff?" asked Alex. "Keep going. Read my favorite part."

"'A bold move by Alex Reel had her playing Princess Winnifred with short, cropped hair. Reel could not have been more energetic, springing to life in Act 2, full of spit and vinegar.'"

"Remind me again why 'full of spit' is a good thing?" Joey asked.

Alex leaned back against the couch and howled.

"Speaking of vinegar, what do you say I hit the kitchen so we can mack on some cupcakes with bomb frosting?" I teased, imitating the glam girls in one of Alex's teen magazines.

"Snack Attack!" said Joey.

"What's that got to do with vinegar?" Alex asked. I didn't dare tell them that even Pink Velvet cupcakes called for my secret ingredient—a dash of vinegar.

On my way back with the positively perfect Pink Velvets, I paused for a moment in the doorway before crossing the threshold to the family room. My sisters were elbow-wrestling and comparing feet and Alex was trying out sparkly clips in Joey's short hair.

Joey chewed on her pencil, probably dreaming up a new list, while Alex twined her necklace around her finger. Comedy and Tragedy were reunited, back where they belonged.

Alex wasn't just Actress. Big Sister. Fink Face. Wicked Witch. Beauty. Green-Eyed Monster. Porcupine. Princess.

She was all of those things.

Joey, too. Jo, J-o-e, Reader, Writer, Little Sister, List-maker, Duck, Funny Girl.

And so was I: Singer. Baker. Sister. Peacemaker.

Watching my sisters, it hit me for the first time in a very long time that I wasn't wishing for things to be the way they used to be. I liked who we were in that moment. *Happy in our own skins.*

As Will himself said, *All's Well That Ends Well.* For a way-old Wise Guy, that guy sure had smarts.

"Drum roll, please," I said, presenting my cupcakes.

"Finally! We get to eat the Make-Up cupcakes." Before you could say Nosey Parker, Joey had pink icing on her nose.

I handed Alex the Princess-and-the-Pea cupcake made especially for her. It had twenty (count them) rainbow stripes of icing for the twenty mattresses in the play, and one green pea sticking out from underneath. And on top, a single candy heart that said, EVER AFTER.

I crawled across the well-loved corduroy couch and plopped down in the middle of my two sisters. The room went quiet for a minute, except for lip-smacking sounds, that is.

"Cupcakes. Oh, aren't cupcakes divinity?" Joey asked, imitating Amy in *Little Women*.

"Question," said Alex, who couldn't help staring at my short hair again. "Don't get me wrong, your hair looks great, but, why—?"

"Why would I chop off my hair *on purpose* if I didn't have to?"

"Exactly," said Alex, cracking up.

Sisterhood, I was thinking as I pulled my sisters in tight. How could I explain it to Alex?

"I can't be the only one around here with Rapunzel hair. How else is everybody going to know we're sisters?"

Knife, Fork, Spoon.

Rock, Paper, Scissors.

It's the Rule of Three.